I glanced over at the waterfall at the far end of the pool.

One of the shade umbrellas that normally stood over the poolside tables appeared to have blown over there and caught on one of the rocks or something, so that it almost completely obscured the view of the picturesque waterfall.

The assistant director glared at the waterfall. "Who put that thing there, anyway? I was told the pool would be ready for this shot! Time is money, people...."

Harvey, the main director, only rolled his eyes. "Relax, Michaels," he told the other man. "We'll have it out of the way in a moment."

Suddenly there was a shout from the far end of the pool. Glancing over there, I saw that the crew member had just wrestled the umbrella out of the way.

That left us all with a clear view of the waterfall—and the graffiti that someone had scrawled across the rock face in bold black letters:

STOP WASTING TIME IN THE SHALLOW
END. LOOK DEEPER BEFORE TIME
RUNS OUT!

NANCY DREW

GIRL DETECTIVE

Available from Aladdin

CAROLYN KEENE

NANCY DREW

GIRL DETECTIVE®

GREEN WITH ENVY

#40

**Book Two in the
Eco Mystery Trilogy**

Aladdin
New York   London   Toronto   Sydney   New Delhi

This book is a work of fiction. Any references to historical events, real people, or real locales are used fictitiously. Other names, characters, places, and incidents are the product of the author's imagination, and any resemblance to actual events or locales or persons, living or dead, is entirely coincidental.

ALADDIN
An imprint of Simon & Schuster Children's Publishing Division
1230 Avenue of the Americas, New York, NY 10020
First Aladdin paperback edition February 2010
Text copyright © 2010 by Simon & Schuster, Inc.
All rights reserved, including the right of reproduction in whole or in part in any form.
ALADDIN is a trademark of Simon & Schuster, Inc., and related logo is a registered trademark of Simon & Schuster, Inc.
NANCY DREW, NANCY DREW: GIRL DECTECTIVE, and related logo are registered trademarks of Simon & Schuster, Inc.
For information about special discounts for bulk purchases, please contact Simon & Schuster Special Sales at 1-866-506-1949 or business@simonandschuster.com.
The Simon & Schuster Speakers Bureau can bring authors to your live event. For more information or to book an event contact the Simon & Schuster Speakers Bureau at 1-866-248-3049 or visit our website at www.simonspeakers.com.
Designed by Sammy Yuen Jr.
The text of this book was set in Bembo.
Manufactured in the United States of America
1014 OFF
10 9 8 7 6 5
Library of Congress Control Number 2009924058
ISBN 978-1-4169-7842-8
ISBN 978-1-4169-9876-1 (eBook)

Contents

CONTENTS

NEW QUESTIONS

It's not every day you walk in to find an enormous dead sea turtle bleeding all over the lobby of the resort where you're staying.

"Please calm down, everyone!" Even as he said it, Cristobal Arrojo looked anything but calm himself. And no wonder. A whole group of us had just walked into the lobby of Casa Verde to find the unfortunate turtle splayed in the middle of the floor in a puddle of blood. I stared at it, not wanting to believe what this meant.

"Whoa. This is bad, Nancy, really bad," my friend

Bess Marvin murmured in my ear, her blue eyes wide and troubled.

Her cousin and my other best friend, George Fayne, just gulped and nodded. Most people think of Bess and George as polar opposites—Bess is blond and curvy and feminine, with a penchant for pretty dresses and high heels; George is a tomboy who would sooner go naked than give up her jeans and sneakers. The truth is, though, they're both pretty tough and no-nonsense under the surface.

But at the moment, both of them were looking a little green around the gills. The three of us have seen some fairly serious crime scenes—back home in River Heights, people like to call me Nancy Drew, Girl Detective, due to my penchant for amateur sleuthing. But most of said crime scenes don't involve actual death and bloodshed.

However, that wasn't the only reason I was feeling slightly queasy myself at the sight of the dead turtle. See, I'd thought we'd already figured out who was causing trouble at Casa Verde. The beautiful Costa Rican eco-resort, a former coffee plantation that had been refurbished from top to bottom to be a model of green living, had been plagued by trouble since the moment we'd arrived. And not the kind of trouble you'd expect due to the fact that it was the resort's opening week, like malfunctioning faucets or whatever. No, this trouble was more along the lines of vandalized luggage and mysterious threatening notes.

"Do you think Juliana could have done this?" George whispered.

I glanced around to make sure nobody was listening to our conversation. No danger of that. Almost all of the other guests that week were reporters and other members of the press who had been invited to cover Casa Verde's grand opening. Most of them were now milling around shouting questions while Cristobal, who co-owned the resort with his brother, Enrique, continued to do his best to calm everyone down.

"I don't know," I said to my friends. "I suppose it's possible it is Juliana causing trouble again. We already know she was willing to go to great lengths to get back at her uncle. But would she really be stupid enough to pull something like this *after* she's been outed?"

Juliana was Enrique Arrojo's daughter. During the first half of our week at Casa Verde, my friends and I had discovered that the Arrojo brothers had a troubled family history. Enrique had fallen in love with and married a woman named Virginia. But Virginia had ended up spending a lot of time with Cristobal, and eventually fell in love with the gregarious older brother. She'd requested an annulment of her marriage to Enrique so she could marry Cristobal, and while Virginia and Cristobal were still blissfully happy, it appeared that Enrique had never really recovered from the betrayal. He remarried, but that relationship had lasted only long enough to produce a daughter, Juliana. At first we'd thought Enrique might be behind the trouble at the resort himself, driven by a desire for revenge, but finally we'd fingered the now-teenage Juliana as the culprit—with the same motive. Could she be behind this latest horrible incident as well?

As I glanced around the room, on the alert for clues, I noticed that eight-year-old Robin Kent was still staring wide-eyed at the turtle. Robin was visiting the resort with her mother, Hildy, a freelance travel writer. The little girl had been the first one to see the dead turtle, and she looked pretty upset.

Somebody else noticed too. "Come, *señorita*," Cristobal crooned, trying to steer the young girl off in the direction of the dining room. "Let's get you out of here, hmm?"

"No, it's okay." Robin's voice wavered a little as she shook Cristobal's hand off her shoulder. She swallowed hard before continuing. "I'm fine now. I was just s-surprised."

"Are you sure?" Cristobal asked.

"She'll be all right," Hildy said firmly. "My daughter is tougher than she looks."

I smiled at Robin, impressed by the little girl's bravery. She was certainly acting more mature than some of the others in the room. For instance, Deirdre Shannon and her cousin Kat. Deirdre was someone my friends and I knew from River Heights. Although we'd gone all through school with her, we couldn't really call her a friend, exactly. Deirdre's the type of person who requires her friends to worship the ground she walks on. None of us do—and we're not the types to fake it. So let's just call her an acquaintance.

In any case, she had won this trip to Casa Verde in a raffle, just like Bess had. While Bess had invited George and me along to share the week, Deirdre had brought her cousin, who lived in California. Kat was nice enough, though much like Deirdre, she rarely talked about anything but herself—her job as an extra in movies, the fancy Hollywood parties she got invited to, the celebrities she'd met. And she never went anywhere without her spoiled Chihuahua, Pretty Boy.

Right now Deirdre was ranting about having her relaxing day ruined by this, while Kat covered Pretty Boy's eyes with one carefully manicured hand and hugged him fiercely to her chest with the other.

"Don't look, baby!" she cried into the little dog's ear. "It's too horrible for your innocent eyes!"

Pretty Boy wriggled against her grip, seeming kind of annoyed. I wasn't sure whether that was because of Kat's current behavior or the ridiculous navy-and-white-striped sailor outfit she'd forced him to wear that day. He let out a series of yaps, then bit Kat on the hand.

"Aw, it's okay, little guy," Kat said, stroking him on his bulbous head as his beady eyes followed her movements, clearly waiting for an opportunity to get another nip in. "I know you're upset. Mommy forgives you, poor baby."

I stepped away from Kat and Deirdre, trying to hear what some of the others were saying. Alicia Alvarez had stepped closer to the turtle for a better view, looking as upset as everyone else. Alicia was a biologist who served as Casa Verde's resident groundskeeper and animal outreach expert. Her forehead wrinkled with confusion as she touched the dead animal's leathery skin.

"*Dios mio*," she said. "Hold on, everyone. Something doesn't look quite right here."

"No kidding," Deirdre snapped. "You know, in all the times Daddy and Mother and I have stayed at five-star hotels and resorts all over the world, nothing like *this* has happened."

Cristobal was usually all about customer relations, even when that customer was acting as obnoxious as Deirdre was. But at the moment, he didn't even seem to hear her comment.

"The sea turtle is an endangered species and a beloved icon here in Costa Rica," he said sadly. "Who would do such a thing to an innocent creature?"

"Alicia, what do you mean by 'Something doesn't look right'?" I asked, carefully keeping my eyes averted from the awful sight. "Can you tell how this turtle was killed?"

"No, but I have some idea about *when* it was killed," the biologist replied matter-of-factly. "And it wasn't any time recently."

Cristobal stepped forward. "What are you talking about?"

"I don't know where all this blood came from." Alicia waved a hand at the crimson stains soaking into the carpet and spattered on the walls and furniture. "But it certainly wasn't from this turtle. See its eyes? They aren't real—the turtle's been stuffed. Looks like some time ago too."

"What are you saying?" Frankie Gillman demanded sharply, clicking forward on her high-heeled sandals. "This is a fake turtle?"

I cringed, remembering the last time Frankie had started shooting questions at Alicia. While investigating the earlier problems, I'd accidentally let Frankie in on the case. She was a reporter for the *New York Globe*, which she seemed to think made her an expert on solving crimes. But in truth she'd almost blown the whole case when she'd aggressively interviewed Alicia and her rather shy young assistant, Sara Sanchez, all but accusing them of being behind all the trouble.

Fortunately, Alicia didn't seem to be holding any grudges about that. "No, not a fake," she told Frankie patiently. "A taxidermy. This leatherback turtle died long ago—perhaps killed before they were protected, or perhaps dying of natural causes. Someone preserved and stuffed its body."

The resort's driver, Pedro, had been gazing at the turtle ever since he'd entered with the rest of us. But now his expression cleared. He turned to Cristobal and let out a torrent of rapid-fire Spanish that I couldn't even begin to follow. I glanced at Bess, who could usually follow along pretty well, thanks to her high school Spanish classes. But she just shrugged helplessly.

"What?" I asked, glancing from Pedro to Cristobal. "What is it?"

Alicia spoke before either of the men could. "Of course!" she exclaimed. "I should have recognized it myself."

"What are you talking about?" Poppy LeVeau demanded. As usual, she looked every inch the fashion magazine writer that she was. Her dark hair was swept into an elegant updo. An expensive-looking sarong was knotted stylishly over the designer bikini she'd worn on that day's outing, a snorkeling trip to a nearby lagoon.

"Pedro just pointed out that this appears to be the same stuffed turtle that's been on display for years in a local restaurant down in San Isidro," Cristobal said, referring to the closest town. "I suppose we should call and see if they are indeed missing this fellow."

"I'll do it." Frankie whipped out a cell phone. "What's the place called?"

As Cristobal gave Frankie the information, George moved closer to me. "Guess the *Globe* must be paying her roaming charges, huh?" she whispered, sounding envious as she eyed Frankie's cell. George was a techno-freak. This trip was really testing her ability to live without her phone, laptop, and other beloved gadgets.

Soon Frankie was snapping her phone shut again. "It's theirs, all right," she reported grimly. "Someone broke into the place last night after closing and took it."

"Wow." George stared at the turtle, which was close to six feet long and probably weighed somewhere in the vicinity of a ton. "Those were some motivated thieves."

Aside from Kat talking to Pretty Boy, the room fell silent for a moment. I wasn't sure whether this latest news made me feel better or worse. On the one hand, it seemed no endangered sea turtles had been harmed in the making of this statement. That was definitely a good thing.

On the other hand, I had no idea what this statement was supposed to be telling us. There was no way Juliana could have moved the huge leatherback on her own. That meant either she had accomplices, or somebody else entirely had done this.

Cristobal sighed loudly. "I'm so sorry for this, er, mishap," he said, finally seeming to recover his usual smooth, friendly demeanor. "Please, if you'd all like to retire to the pool area, I'll see that Enrique brings you some refreshing snacks to enjoy while we get things cleaned up in here."

With that, he hurried over to the phone on the lobby desk and started making calls. The others slowly drifted off, though only Deirdre, Kat, and Pretty Boy actually disappeared through the door leading toward the pool. Frankie hung around in the main part of the lobby, staring thoughtfully at the turtle, while Poppy, Hildy, and Robin chatted over near the dining room doors, all of them looking perplexed.

Meanwhile, another door opened and two people entered. The first was Sarene Neuman, Frankie's friend who'd accompanied her on this trip. Sarene was a writer who had won a National Book Award for a recent nonfiction book about the life cycle of salmon. I wasn't sure why she'd bothered to come to Casa Verde, since she seemed to find many of the resort's activities insufficiently environmentally correct for her tastes. She'd even skipped that day's snorkeling, announcing at breakfast that gawking at exotic sea creatures while potentially damaging the reefs they rely on for life was just as bad as dumping toxic waste down their throats. Or something like that, anyway.

Now Sarene's cool green eyes widened slightly as she took in the sight of the bloody turtle. She immediately headed over to Frankie, and soon the two of them were deep in conversation.

The second person who entered was Sara, Alicia's assistant. "There you are!" Alicia greeted her. "Don't worry, it's not what it looks like. . . ." She switched to Spanish for a moment.

Sara nodded, her gaze sweeping over the turtle and the blood. "I just heard," she said. "Señor Arrojo called the employee lounge, wanting us all to come immediately."

Indeed, several other resort employees soon arrived and got to work scrubbing up the mess on

11

the carpets and walls. Alicia and Sara moved around the turtle itself, carefully cleaning the blood off its shell and body.

My friends and I huddled in a quiet spot behind a potted palm to discuss the situation. "Well?" George said grimly, sweeping a hand through her close-cropped dark hair. "What do we do now?"

"I'm not sure." I bit my lip and looked over at the turtle. "Obviously if Juliana's behind this, she had help."

"Well, we can rule out everyone who was on the snorkeling trip," Bess pointed out. "That includes Cristobal, Alicia, and most of the guests."

"But not Sarene," I said, glancing toward the writer. "Or Poppy's boyfriend, Adam, either."

"True." Bess winced. "That sounded like quite a fight those two had before breakfast this morning."

"Yeah." We'd all heard Poppy and Adam's argument through the dining-room windows. It had sounded pretty bitter, and I don't think anyone was surprised when Adam had begged off the snorkeling trip, claiming he didn't feel well.

George frowned. "Look, what's the point in worrying about everyone else's alibis?" she said. "If Juliana was behind this, she can tell us who helped her."

"But do you really think she'd do something like this?" Bess asked.

"Why wouldn't she?" George countered. "She's the one who snatched that oversize mosquito of Kat's, right? We caught her red-handed."

That was true enough. During an earlier excursion someone had slipped some animal tranquilizer into Pedro the driver's water bottle, which he'd sipped from while he was waiting for us on the bus with Pretty Boy. When we'd returned, the driver had been unconscious and the Chihuahua had vanished. We'd tracked down Pretty Boy a couple of days later in Juliana's private study room, which had been the conclusive evidence that she was our culprit.

"Then there's the note," George added.

I'd almost forgotten about that. When we'd first walked in and seen the bloody scene today, we'd also spotted a note sitting on top of the turtle's shell. In big block letters it had read:

I TOLD YOU TO LOOK DEEPER. HOW MUCH MONEY HAS CASA VERDE TAKEN FROM THE GOVERNMENT, ONLY TO HURT WHAT THEY ARE SUPPOSED TO CONSERVE! UNLESS YOU WANT MORE ANIMALS TO SUFFER LIKE THIS, FIND THE TRUTH!!

The paper and writing seemed identical to several similar notes that had appeared at Casa Verde since our arrival. Now that I remembered this latest note,

I started walking over to see if I could take another look. But it was gone.

"I think Frankie grabbed it," George said, guessing what I was thinking. "But I got a pretty good look before she did. The writing style matches the earlier notes. The stationery, too. So that looks like a big duh to me—it had to be Juliana."

"But isn't she supposed to be in school all day today?" Bess said.

Just then there was a murmur from the employees and guests around the lobby. Glancing up, I saw that Enrique Arrojo had just entered carrying a tray of food and drinks. Judging by the expressions on most of the other faces, it seemed my friends and I weren't the only ones thinking his daughter might be responsible for this latest mischief.

"Listen, I think I'd better talk to Juliana," I said, hurrying toward a courtesy phone on a bamboo end table nearby. George was right—Juliana did seem like a slam dunk as the culprit for this incident too. But something about the whole situation was bugging me. "If she's supposed to be in school today, it should be easy enough to check her alibi for the time when this was done."

"Want me to talk to her?" Bess offered. "I know we were all there when you busted her, but . . ."

"That's a good idea." I dialed Juliana's cell phone

number, then handed the phone to Bess. "She might be more likely to talk to you."

Bess is probably the most diplomatic person I know. She greeted Juliana kindly, asking how she was doing. Within moments the two of them were chatting like old friends.

Unfortunately, George and I could only hear Bess's side of the conversation, which was kind of frustrating. Bess didn't mention the turtle, but she did ask if Juliana was in school that day. Actually, she said, "I hope I'm not interrupting one of your classes or anything."

She paused to listen to whatever Juliana said in response. Her eyebrows lifted a little.

"Oh, really?" she said, glancing at us.

"What?" George muttered.

"Shh!" I warned.

Bess was listening again. She didn't say much else except for a couple more "Oh, really's" and some "hmm's" and "I see's." Then she added, "Would you mind if I spoke to her for a second?"

George and I traded a look. Who was "her"? A teacher?

Soon Bess was introducing herself to whomever was on the other end of the line as "a friend of Juliana's." "I just wanted to thank you for being so kind," she added. After listening for another moment, she added, "Well, it certainly sounds like you two made a lot of progress today."

I tapped my foot impatiently. Luckily, Bess seemed to be winding things down. After a little more small talk she hung up and turned to us.

"That was interesting," she said.

"What?" George demanded. "Who was that? Was Juliana in school today?"

"Not exactly." Bess glanced over at Enrique and Cristobal, who were doing their best to shoo the others out of the lobby. "You know how she and her father and uncle have started family counseling over what happened?"

I nodded. "Of course."

"Well, I guess the counselor got permission to take Juliana out of school to go to some workshop for troubled teens or something like that today." Bess shrugged. "The workshop started at eight this morning, and just finished up a few minutes ago. Oh, and it was in San Jose."

My eyes widened. San Jose was over three hours' drive from Casa Verde.

"Given that the turtle wasn't here yet when we left the resort at nine," I said slowly, "I guess that means there's no way Juliana could have done it."

NO ANSWERS

Before my friends could say anything else, Cristobal came bustling toward us. "Please, friends," he said in his charming way, "would it be possible for you to go out and enjoy the pool or other amenities? The staff and I would really love to have things cleaned up in here before dinnertime."

"Sure, no problem." I glanced at the turtle, now more curious than ever about how it had ended up there. But any possible clues were probably long gone, thanks to the clean-up crew, so I allowed myself to be swept out the lobby's side door along with the other guests.

"Well, *that* was upsetting," Poppy commented as we all wandered along the manicured, flower-lined path toward the pool area.

Frankie nodded and looked at me. "Looks like the problems at Casa Verde aren't over after all, despite all my work to expose that Juliana troublemaker."

I just smiled blandly in response. Even though my friends and I were the ones who'd figured out most of the mystery, Frankie had managed to take almost full credit for it. She'd even published an article about it already in the *Globe*. I didn't care too much about that sort of thing, but she'd also come close to messing things up with her aggressive, impulsive interview style. I didn't want that to happen again.

"I think I got a little too much sun today," I announced to the group at large. "I'd better go back to the room and put on some aloe or something before dinner."

I shot my friends a meaningful look. They both caught on right away.

"I'll come too," Bess said. "I want to change shoes."

"Uh, me too." George hurried along after us as we left the pool area.

But we didn't bother going all the way back to our room. As soon as we were out of sight and earshot of the others, we stopped to talk.

"So?" George asked me. "Any theories yet?"

I shook my head. "I suppose it's still possible Juliana is involved," I said. "She could be working with an accomplice. Maybe another resort employee, or someone from town . . ."

"That's true," Bess agreed. "It could even be the reason the turtle thing happened today. They could have planned it that way, because it would mean she had a built-in alibi for the time it was planted in the lobby."

"But not for the time it was stolen," George pointed out. "At least if Frankie was right about it being taken in the dead of night."

"Maybe we should follow up on that angle," I said, already looking around for a phone.

I started walking toward an information hut, where guests could pick up maps of the nature trails. Maybe there was a phone in there. But just then we heard the sound of voices from somewhere just around the corner. Loud, complaining voices.

A moment later, Deirdre and her cousin appeared. Kat was carrying Pretty Boy, as usual.

"Oh! There you are, Nancy." Kat rushed up to me. She was close enough that Pretty Boy seemed to be eyeing me hungrily.

"Hello," I said, taking a step backward out of nipping range. "What's up?"

"Deirdre has been telling me all about how you're this superfabulous detective back home," Kat began eagerly.

Deirdre frowned. "That's not what I said," she put in. "I said she's always nosing around in stuff that's none of her business. And once in a while she actually stumbles upon a mystery or something."

Kat waved away her cousin's correction. "Whatever. My point is, Nancy, you just have to figure out who did this horrible thing!" she exclaimed. "It's just soooo upsetting. Who knows what else someone like that might do? They might even dognap Pretty Boy again!" She hugged the little dog to her chest. He growled, looking annoyed.

"It was probably the chef-owner guy's daughter." Deirdre examined her manicure. "She did the other stuff, right? Frankie figured it all out."

"Frankie?" George put in, sounding annoyed.

Kat was still hugging Pretty Boy. "Whoever did it, I just know that Pretty Boy and I won't sleep well until he or she is behind bars!" she shrieked. "Not after what happened last time!"

She was being pretty melodramatic, but I suppose you couldn't blame her. After having her beloved dog go missing for a couple of days, she was probably still suffering from PTDS—post-traumatic dognapping syndrome. Although from the looks of Pretty Boy's expression, it seemed he wouldn't mind a little more separation at the moment. He finally let out a yip and snapped at Kat's finger, missing by a fraction of an inch.

Just then we heard the sound of Cristobal's voice calling the guests to dinner. "Come on," I said. "We'd better head in."

Halfway back to the dining room, we ran into Frankie and Sarene. "Hello, girls," Frankie greeted us, her gaze fixed on me. "Talking about what happened in there?"

You didn't have to be a detective to see that she was fishing for information. Even if she'd taken all the credit for outing Juliana, it seemed she might actually have some clue that I'd done most of the work.

Once again, tactful Bess came to the rescue. "Oh no, we just want to forget all about that," she said with a chuckle. "We were trying to remember how many different kinds of fish we saw while we were snorkeling today."

Sarene looked sour. "Did you also count up how much of the irreplaceable coral reef you destroyed by floundering around out there for your own amusement?"

Deirdre rolled her eyes. "This one must be a blast at cocktail parties," she muttered.

"What was that?" Sarene demanded, eyeing Deirdre suspiciously.

"Wow, I just realized how hungry I am," I piped in loudly, not wanting to let any sniping start. "Snorkeling really builds up your appetite. Let's get in there and eat!"

"Thanks for the ride, Violeta," I said as I hopped out of the cramped car belonging to Casa Verde's staff nurse. Bess and George climbed out as well.

"You are most welcome, girls." Violeta nodded at us. "It should take me about an hour to finish my errands here in town. Will that be enough time?"

"That's fine," Bess told her with a smile. "We just want to poke around San Isidro a little bit. We'll meet you back here."

Dinner had ended half an hour earlier. My friends and I had been lucky enough to overhear Violeta telling Cristobal that she had to run into town for a little while, and we had begged a ride with her. That way we could go in person to check out the restaurant where the turtle had been stolen, rather than relying on a phone call that might be hampered by the iffy lines or our weak grasp of Spanish.

"Do you have the address?" George asked as soon as Violeta was out of earshot.

I nodded and pulled a slip of paper out of my shorts pocket. "It shouldn't be too far from here."

As it turned out, the restaurant was easy to find—not least because one of Casa Verde's service trucks had just pulled up in front of it. The stuffed sea turtle was visible through the slatted sides around the back.

"Wow, Cristobal doesn't waste any time," George commented as we stepped closer.

We weren't the only ones who'd noted the truck's arrival. People started pouring out of the restaurant, calling out to the resort employees in Spanish. In addition, passersby gathered curiously around, jostling one another and craning their necks for a better view. It seemed word traveled fast around town—within moments there was quite a crowd surrounding the place.

"Guess interviewing the restaurant owner will have to wait," I told my friends with a sigh.

We watched as Pedro and several other resort employees wrestled the turtle to the edge of the truck bed. Half a dozen other men joined them to help lower it carefully to the ground.

Another man, older than the others, came forward to examine the turtle. His expression went dark as he pointed to something on its back and let loose with some angry-sounding Spanish.

"What's that all about?" George asked.

I shrugged, glancing at Bess. She was leaning forward, listening carefully.

"It sounds like he's saying the turtle is damaged?" she said uncertainly. "I don't know some of the vocabulary, but something about a piece being missing?"

I took a step closer, peering between a couple of teenage girls who were watching and chattering excitedly in Spanish themselves. At first I couldn't see anything wrong with the turtle—in fact, I was impressed by how well Alicia and Sara had cleaned it up, leaving no trace of all that blood.

But then one of the men who'd lifted it down stepped aside, and I saw what the other man must be talking about. "There!" I told my friends, pointing. "It looks like part of the shell is missing. Maybe it got broken off by whoever stole it."

"More like ripped off," Bess corrected. "That's a leatherback, right? That means its shell is softer than most turtles."

"Broken, ripped, whatever." George shrugged and watched the older man gesture wildly as he yelled at Pedro and the others. "Seems like they're pretty upset about it."

Just then I noticed one of the restaurant workers, a wiry man in his twenties, wandering closer. "*Habla Ingles?*" I asked him.

24

He stopped and looked at me. "Yes, a little bit," he said. "How can I help you? Are you young ladies looking for a fine place to enjoy a meal this evening?"

"I'm afraid not—we already ate." I smiled at him, glad to hear that his English actually seemed pretty good. "We were just wondering if you know who might have stolen that turtle from the restaurant last night."

The young man's face darkened. "I do not," he said. "It happened late last night when we had all gone home. The only traces left of the terrible crime were some tire tracks in the mud." He gestured to the area in front of the restaurant's doors.

"Are you sure there wasn't anything else?" I asked. "Did the police—"

Before I could finish, someone over at the truck called out sharply. The young man excused himself and hurried back to the group.

"Tire tracks, eh?" George glanced around at the ground, which was muddy and soft. "Think we should take a look?"

I nodded. "We'll have to wait, though."

The group over by the Casa Verde truck was gathering around the sea turtle again. We watched as they hoisted it up and carried it toward the restaurant. Judging by the sweat pouring off their brows and the expressions on their faces, the turtle was just as heavy as I'd guessed. But finally, after much grunting and what sounded like quite a few Spanish curses and complaints, they got it safely inside.

"Come on," I said as Pedro and most of the other Casa Verde workers disappeared into the restaurant. "Let's look for those tracks."

We hurried over. Unfortunately, there wasn't much to see. Whatever marks had been there must have been covered by the tracks of the Casa Verde truck, since those were the only tracks we could see.

There were still plenty of onlookers gathered around. I tried to question a few of them, but most didn't speak much or any English. Finally I spotted the young man from earlier emerging from the restaurant.

"Excuse me," I said, rushing over to him. "Is everything okay now? Did you guys get the turtle safely back into place?"

The young man nodded, mopping his brow with a handkerchief. "Yes, it is back where it belongs," he said, shooting a dark look at the Casa Verde truck. "No thanks to Señor Arrojo."

"You mean Cristobal?" I traded a quick look with my friends. "You don't think he had anything to do with the theft, do you?"

The man shrugged. "All I know is that he tried to

buy the turtle from my boss a month or two ago," he said. "My boss, he said no."

"You mean Cristobal wanted to buy the sea turtle from this restaurant?" George put in. "What happened, he didn't offer enough money?"

"Oh, he offered plenty," the man said. "But the turtle is not for sale. There is not enough money to replace its value to us." He shrugged again. "Though some would disagree, of course."

"What do you mean? Who would disagree?" I asked.

The young man shot a slightly guilty look around him. "Pay no attention to me," he said with a forced-sounding laugh. "It is only the boss's wife, she thought the extra money could be useful to expand the restaurant. You know—to allow for the extra tourists that Casa Verde will bring to our town." He shook his head. "Then again, she is not from San Isidro by birth, so she does not understand that some of us do not care for having such a resort changing our town."

Interesting. As the young man excused himself and hurried away, I pondered what he'd just said.

"Wow," Bess said. "Sounds like Casa Verde might be a little controversial with the locals."

Before George or I could respond, a woman came rushing up to the group, yelling and pumping her fist.

She really stood out among the mostly lean, dark-haired locals. Her overprocessed blond hair stood out around her round, sunburned face like a clown wig, and her pudgy body was stuffed into a polyester sundress that was dotted with pins proclaiming her membership in various environmental groups.

"This just proves that Casa not-so-Verde can't be trusted!" she shouted in an accent straight out of the American Midwest. "Stealing already-dead endangered turtles is the least of that place's abuses!"

Pedro and the others were still inside, but the two Casa Verde employees who'd been left behind lounging against the truck stood up straight when they saw her. As the woman continued shouting, the employees muttered to each other. Then the older of the pair stepped forward.

"You stay away!" he ordered in heavily accented English. "We do not need your sort here. Casa Verde, it is a good place."

"Good?" The woman let out a loud snort. "Good at making money, maybe. Being environmentally conscious? Not hardly!"

"Wow, she seems pretty worked up," Bess murmured. "Wonder who she is?"

"One way to find out." I started toward the woman. But I was too late. The Casa Verde employees chased her off, still yelling at her to stay away from the resort.

By the time I reached them, they were muttering under their breath in Spanish. "Everything all right?" I asked.

The older one blinked as he recognized me. "*Buenas tardes, señorita*," he said with a polite little nod. "*Sí*, everything it is fine. It is only a troublemaker."

I tried to ask who the woman was and why they'd looked so angry about seeing her. But I didn't get any answers. I wasn't sure if the employees were pretending not to understand English to avoid my questions or if they really didn't understand me.

Either way, I soon gave up. "Come on," I told my friends. "Let's see if we can find that woman."

"Do you really think she knows anything?" George looked dubious. "Seemed kind of like the rabble-rousing type to me."

I shrugged. "Can't hurt to talk to her and find out."

We wandered around that part of San Isidro for the next few minutes. But there was no sign of the wild-haired American woman anywhere. When we returned to the restaurant, the Casa Verde truck had disappeared as well.

"It's almost time to meet Violeta," Bess said, checking her watch.

I sighed. "Let's go. We're not getting any useful leads here, anyway."

During the bumpy ride back to Casa Verde on the rutted, curvy local roads, I thought over what we'd just witnessed. Who was that woman? Did she really know anything about Casa Verde, or was she just a nut? Then there was what that local man had said. Could there be people in town who were holding a grudge against the resort? If so, how were my friends and I ever going to track them down—especially since we were only going to be in Costa Rica for another couple of days?

Deciding not to worry about that at the moment, I turned my thoughts next to the suspects at Casa Verde itself. It seemed suspicious that Cristobal had tried to purchase that very turtle, though I couldn't imagine what he'd stand to gain by stealing it in such a public way. Enrique was another potential suspect. Could he be trying to frame his brother or something like that? And, of course, there was still the possibility that Juliana was involved somehow, despite her alibi.

Speaking of alibis, there were a couple of guests who didn't have one. Poppy's boyfriend, Adam, and Sarene had been at the resort when the turtle had appeared in the lobby. They weren't the only ones, though. As far as I knew, Enrique didn't have an alibi either. For that matter, the only resort employees who did were Cristobal, Pedro, and Alicia—and all three of them had accompanied us on the snorkeling trip.

By the time we pulled in through Casa Verde's front gates, I hadn't reached any useful conclusions. My friends and I thanked Violeta as she dropped us off in front of the lobby. While we were climbing out of the car, a monkey screeched somewhere in the darkening jungle nearby.

A moment later, an ear-shattering and much louder scream came from just inside the lobby. And the second scream was definitely human!

HAVING WORDS

"What was that?" George exclaimed.

I was already running for the door. "Come on!"

But when my friends and I skidded to a stop inside the lobby, there was no sign of any murder or mayhem—or even any more bloody turtles. All we saw was Kat and Deirdre shrieking with excitement and dancing around like idiots. Pretty Boy was prancing at his mistress's feet, clearly picking up on her mood.

"What's going on?" Bess called out, hurrying toward them.

Deirdre waved one of the resort phones around as she responded. "This is so awesome!" she cried gleefully. "And just when I thought nothing on this stupid trip was going to go right!"

"I know, right?" Kat squealed, scooping up Pretty Boy and spinning around with him. "It's soooo amazing!"

I exchanged a mystified look with my friends. Usually the only thing that got Deirdre this excited was a big sale at the mall. Or maybe getting in a good zinger against George.

"So what's the amazing news?" I asked loudly.

It took a few more tries, but finally Kat heard us. She stopped dancing and shrieking long enough to answer.

"We just found out that Green Solutions is sending a crew to Casa Verde to film an ad spot for their website!" she exclaimed, setting Pretty Boy down on the floor at her feet.

"Green Solutions?" George echoed. "You mean the environmental consulting company that helped design and build this place?"

"Aren't they an American company?" I asked. George had done some research on Green Solutions before our trip. It was a fairly new company that specialized in helping other businesses "go green." Its headquarters was in Chicago, not terribly far from our own hometown of River Heights, though I had to admit I'd never heard of the company before Bess had won the trip.

"Who cares where they're from?" Deirdre rolled her eyes. "The point is, when they found out Kat has extensive acting experience, they naturally insisted she star in the ads."

"Along with my beautiful cousin, of course," Kat added, hugging Deirdre. When Pretty Boy yapped and nipped at her ankle, she giggled and swept him up again into the hug. "And my gorgeous baby boy will surely get a featured role as soon as they see him!"

Deirdre waved away the little dog, who had started chewing on her curly dark hair. "We're just lucky they're getting here before we leave," she added.

"Yeah." Kat's face fell slightly. "I hope they can get the footage they need in just two days. Otherwise, maybe we should think about extending our stay. . . ."

As the two of them kept chattering, I glanced at my friends. George rolled her eyes, and Bess looked amused. I knew how they felt. As far as we could tell, Kat's "extensive acting experience" mostly consisted of walk-on nonspeaking roles in minor films and low-rated sitcoms. Still, I had to admit she talked a pretty good game. It was no wonder she'd convinced the Green Solutions people that she was a pro.

But I didn't waste much time thinking about that. I was more worried about what the arrival of a film crew would do to our investigation. I'd learned during a recent case involving a hastily planned wedding and an out-of-control reality show that having a bunch of cameras following your every move could really get in the way.

"So the crew is coming tomorrow?" I asked, interrupting Kat and Deirdre's breathless discussion, which by now had shifted to the topic of what they were going to wear for their big debut.

Kat nodded. "Bright and early," she sang out. "That reminds me, I'd better get ready to turn in. Pretty Boy and I want to be sure we get plenty of beauty sleep!"

She, Deirdre, and Pretty Boy hurried off in the direction of their room. "She's going to bed now?" Bess checked her watch. "It's barely eight o'clock."

George shrugged. "It probably takes a while to sand off all that makeup she wears," she said. "Not to mention Deirdre needing to fluff up the pillows in her coffin and check for wooden stakes around the room."

"Never mind," I said. "Film crew or no film crew, we don't have any time to waste. Let's go see if we can find Cristobal. I have a few questions for him."

• • •

"Finally!" I muttered, spotting Cristobal on the far side of the pool near the tumbling waterfall. I'd been looking all over for him. My friends and I had started out by checking his office, which was empty, along with the rest of the lobby.

Then we had been peeking into the kitchen when Hildy and Robin had walked up. They had been on their way to the lounge just off the lobby for the evening's entertainment, a brief film and talk about the local wildlife, hosted by Alicia and Sara. Robin had been so excited about the presentation that Bess hadn't been able to resist agreeing when the little girl had invited us to sit with them, and George had been dragged along as well. I'd only escaped by using the aloe excuse again.

For a while I'd regretted the decision to miss the show. The film had sounded interesting, and I never got tired of learning about the region's flora and fauna. But I felt better when I finally spotted Cristobal. It was starting to get dark by now, and the solar-powered lights in the pool area illuminated his familiar figure.

He wasn't alone. Enrique was with him, and the two of them were involved in what appeared to be an intense conversation. Both men were frowning, and Cristobal was waving his arms around expressively.

What's that all about? I wondered, taking a step forward.

Unfortunately, the rain forest's nighttime sounds—calling birds, chirping and whirring insects, screeching monkeys—were getting louder as the light faded. Between that and the sound of the pool's waterfall, I couldn't hear the men at all.

But after a moment I did hear another pair of voices. It was Poppy and Adam. The two of them had just stepped out of the spa building together, though they looked anything but relaxed.

"Are you kidding me?" Adam spit out as they came closer. "You've made it pretty clear that you have your own separate agenda here, babe. Trust me."

Poppy opened her mouth to answer, but just then she spotted me. Her face went blank.

"Forget it, Adam," she muttered.

"What?" Adam exclaimed. "But I—"

Poppy elbowed him sharply, and he finally noticed me standing there. He pasted a rather weak-looking smile on his face.

"Good evening, Nancy," he called out. "Nice night, isn't it?"

Then the two of them turned and hurried off down a side trail. I shrugged as I watched them go. That had been a little weird. Then again, the two of them *seemed* a little weird. For a couple on a romantic getaway, they sure didn't seem like they were having much fun together.

Once again, I remembered that Adam didn't have an alibi for the turtle incident. Could he be sabotaging the resort for some reason, either with Poppy's help or behind her back? Could that be what they had been fighting about?

I filed the idea away for further thought, though I had to admit it was a weak theory at best. It seemed much more likely that this was still tied in somehow to the whole Arrojo family drama.

That reminded me why I was there. I turned to glance across the pool. Enrique had disappeared while I had been distracted by Poppy and Adam, but Cristobal was still standing there, staring into the clear water.

I hurried around the edge of the pool to join him. "*Buenas noches*," I said. "Do you have a moment? I have a few questions."

His somber expression immediately disappeared, replaced by his usual jovial smile. "Certainly, *señorita*," he said. "I am always glad to be of service."

Despite his polite and attentive words, I couldn't help but notice that his gaze was already wandering. I wanted to come out and ask him what he and his brother had been discussing, since the conversation had clearly left him distracted and upset. But I figured that wasn't the most tactful way to start off.

Instead I asked about his alleged offer to buy the sea turtle. He nodded immediately.

"Yes, I made Señor Vargas what I believed to be a very fair offer," he confirmed. "I thought the stuffed turtle would make a beautiful and fitting centerpiece for the lobby."

"But he turned you down?" I prompted.

Cristobal shrugged. "Yes, but it is no matter. Casa Verde's lobby is beautiful as it is, and I understand his reasons for not wishing to sell."

"You do? What are they, if you don't mind my asking?"

If he was surprised by my pushiness, he hid it pretty well. "I am from this area and understand matters of local pride and such," he said. "So as I say, I understand why he decided against the sale, even if his change of heart was rather sudden."

That didn't really answer my question. But Cristobal's gaze was wandering again, so I decided I'd better move on.

"I saw your brother here a moment ago," I said, doing my best to keep my voice casual. "He must be terribly distraught over all that unpleasantness with Juliana."

"I suppose so." Cristobal blinked, suddenly taking a step away. "Alicia!" he called out to the biologist, who had just hurried into view nearby. "Is everything all right? I thought you would be in the lounge doing your presentation."

Alicia looked up and saw us. "Sara is handling it for me," she replied breathlessly. "I was called away because one of the guests thought she saw an injured coati near one of the trails."

"Did you find anything?" Cristobal asked with concern.

Alicia shrugged. "I was just on my way out there to have a look."

"If you will excuse me, Nancy, I'd better help look into this." Cristobal shot me an apologetic smile, then turned to hurry after the biologist. They both disappeared into the darkening jungle beyond the pool lights.

I stood there for a moment feeling unsatisfied. I still had no idea what the Arrojo brothers had been arguing about just now. Did it have something to do with the old love triangle—or perhaps something more recent, like Juliana's antics?

When I felt a mosquito chomp on my arm, I snapped out of my thoughts. Hurrying inside, I found my friends just emerging from the evening's educational presentation.

"Wow, you missed it, Nancy," Bess exclaimed. "Sara's talk was great!"

George nodded. "She always seems so shy—I wasn't sure she'd even be able to speak in front of a group. But once she got going, she totally got into it."

"She's really passionate about animals and all the environmental stuff," Bess added. "No wonder she ended up working in a place like this!"

"That's nice," I said, barely hearing them. "But listen, I just talked to Cristobal. . . ."

Pulling them aside to a private spot, I filled them in on what little I'd learned. George rolled her eyes when she heard about Poppy and Adam's latest argument.

"I wonder why those two are even together?" she said. "They don't seem to get along too well."

Bess grinned. "Forget about them. I'm more interested in hearing that Cristobal and Enrique were arguing. I wonder if it has anything to do with those love letters."

"I almost forgot about that," I said. Juliana had told us that her father had written numerous love letters on his computer. She was convinced they were unsent letters to Virginia, though she'd also admitted she hadn't gotten a good-enough look to tell for certain.

"What if Enrique's been sending those letters after all, maybe as e-mails?" Bess went on. "Cristobal might have seen them on her computer, or maybe Virginia showed them to him."

"Okay." George shrugged. "But even if that's true, what does it have to do with the turtle incident?"

"I'm not sure." I sighed. "I just wish we had more time here to solve this! But with that film crew arriving tomorrow . . ."

"I know." George grimaced. "I'm already having flashbacks to all that business with cousin Syd's crazy reality-show wedding."

"Never mind. Nancy managed to crack that case, cameras and all," Bess reminded us. "She'll solve this one too."

It was nice to know that my friends had faith in me. But as I climbed into bed later that night, I wasn't feeling nearly as confident. I lay awake long after both my friends were asleep, listening to George's soft snoring and thinking about the case.

I'd just finally dropped off when the room phone rang. For one bleary, confused moment I thought it was morning already and wondered which of my friends had requested a wake-up call.

But then my head cleared and I realized it was still the middle of the night. I heard Bess groan and turn over as the phone rang again.

I reached out and grabbed it, still feeling a bit confused. "Hello?" I mumbled.

"Go to the white water," a voice whispered.

That woke me up a little. I sat up in bed. "What?" I said, pressing the phone to my ear. "Who is this?"

"Go to the white water," the whispering voice

insisted again. "Go right now if you want to look deeper into what Casa Verde is all about!"

"Who are you?" I asked again.

But it was too late. With a *click* the line went dead.

WATERY WEIRDNESS

Now I was really awake. *Go to the white water ...*
I immediately thought back to a nature walk
earlier in the week. Alicia had been guiding
the walk, and she'd pointed out a certain spot in the
river that ran through Casa Verde's nature preserve,
mentioning that it would soon be the launch point
for white-water rafting. The rafts had already been
there, but she had explained that the resort was still
waiting for some permits before they could allow
guests on the river. Could that be what the mysterious caller was talking about?

Carefully sliding out of bed, I reached for my

clothes, planning to grab them and pull them on outside so I wouldn't wake my friends. But just as my hand closed over my hiking boots, a light clicked on.

"Okay, what was that phone call all about?" Bess mumbled, yawning and rubbing her eyes. "And where do you think you're going?"

"Hey!" George grumbled hoarsely without moving in her own bed. "Turn off the light."

"Wake up," Bess told her, sounding more alert with every passing moment. "Nancy's trying to sneak out without us again."

I smiled sheepishly. "Guess I'm busted," I admitted. A few days earlier, I'd tiptoed out of the room to snoop around Cristobal's office in the middle of the night. My friends hadn't known a thing about it until I'd told them the next day.

George rolled over and groaned again. "What time is it?" she complained. "Did I hear the phone ring?"

"As a matter of fact, you did...." I told them about the mysterious caller.

George didn't respond, and I wasn't completely sure she hadn't fallen asleep again. But Bess was sitting straight up in bed, looking wide-awake.

"Who was it, Nancy?" she asked. "Did you recognize the voice?"

I shook my head. "I'm pretty sure it was female; that's all I can tell you," I said. "She kept it to a whisper."

"'Go to the white water,'" Bess quoted thoughtfully. "Do you think she meant the rapids along that one nature trail?"

"That's where I was going to check," I said.

Bess's eyes widened in alarm. "On your own?" she demanded. "Are you crazy? Mysterious whispering criminals aside, it's really not safe to go tromping out into the rain forest on your own in the middle of the night! What if you got bitten by a coral snake? Or squeezed by a boa constrictor?"

"Let me guess," I joked weakly. "Were snakes a big part of that environmental lecture you went to tonight?"

Bess didn't look amused. "This is no time for jokes," she said sternly. "If you're going out there, George and I are coming with you. Right, George?"

"Mmmph, wha?" George mumbled from beneath the covers.

Bess jumped out of bed and hurried over to give her cousin a sharp poke on the shoulder. "Get up," she commanded. "We've got some investigating to do."

Soon all three of us were tiptoeing away from the building. Well, Bess and I were tiptoeing. George was dragging along behind us, complaining and yawning all the way.

We hurried across the manicured grounds toward

the edge of the jungle. I'd grabbed a flashlight on my way out of the room, and I clicked it on as soon as we entered the tree line. Even so, it was pretty dark and spooky out there. The nighttime noises were deafening once we left the serene openness of the resort proper, and I kept catching glimpses of gleaming eyes peering out at us as we passed. It takes a lot to spook me. I'd faced down hardened criminals and dangerous situations with nary a shiver of fear. But the deeper we hiked into the wilds of the rain forest, the farther we got from civilization, the more vulnerable I felt. We'd been assured that it was highly unlikely we'd ever spy a jaguar outside of a zoo, but right then I had to wonder. Every time a frog croaked or a monkey howled, my heart jumped into my throat.

"This is crazy," George said after we'd been walking for a few minutes. She sounded a little more awake by then. "What are we supposed to be doing out here, anyway?"

"Looking deeper, I guess." I played the flashlight beam over the path ahead. Bess's mention of snakes had reminded me that we really did need to be careful out here. Just ahead, the trail we were following split in two.

"I think it's that way," Bess said, pointing to the right.

She was right. After another ten minutes we could hear the river up ahead, even over the cacophony of jungle sounds all around us.

Soon we were standing on the bank overlooking the rushing water. "Well?" George said, smothering a yawn. "Now what?"

"I'm not sure." I cast the flashlight beam here and there, looking for any clues. But all I could see were the beached rafts and a half-built supply hut nearby.

The roar of the tumbling white water drowned out much of the jungle noise. But we could still hear the occasional cry of a monkey or bird.

"Did you hear that?" Bess said after a particularly forlorn cry.

When I shone the flashlight on her, she looked puzzled. "Hear what?" I asked.

"That bird call. I think . . ." She trailed off, tilting her head thoughtfully to one side as the cry came again. "That's weird."

"Everything out here is weird." George wrinkled her nose. "It's probably just some bizarre new breed of monkeys talking about whether they should try to eat us."

"No, I'm serious," Bess said. "That was no monkey. I'm pretty sure that was the call of a common loon."

I shrugged, not too interested in playing Name That Bird Call at the moment. "So what?"

"So there are no loons around here," Bess insisted. "At least I'm pretty sure there aren't. They live much farther north in colder climates. So it seems pretty unlikely we're actually hearing one here in Costa Rica."

"What are you saying?" George asked. "Are we hallucinating? Or do you think Kat brought her beloved pet loon along as well as that flea-bitten little rat of hers?"

But I was staring at Bess by now, catching on. "Are you sure that was a loon call?" I asked, though I knew the answer before she nodded. If Bess said something like that, you could be pretty sure it was true. And she knew a lot of weird and unexpected stuff.

Just then the distinctive call rang out again. "I think it came from over there," Bess said, pointing downriver.

George had caught on by now too. "Do you think it's our mysterious caller?" she hissed as we turned to hurry in the direction of the call.

"It must be," I whispered back, catching myself just in time to keep from tripping over an exposed root. "Hurry! We don't want to lose her."

None of us could spare any attention or energy on talking for the next few minutes. It was all we could do to follow the loon calls, which continued at sporadic intervals. Before long we'd left the trail far behind, instead pushing through virgin jungle. Vines and rough leaves scratched my bare arms, and various insects landed on me, bit me, or got tangled in my hair. Once I had to duck as a bat, presumably confused by my flashlight, almost bombed right into us.

"I'm starting to remember why I never liked camping," George grumbled breathlessly, slapping at a mosquito—or something—as we burst out of the trees into another open area.

Once again, we found ourselves overlooking the river. Or at least *a* river.

"Wait, I thought we were moving away from the river for that last bit?" Bess commented as we stepped forward.

"I'm guessing this is a tributary of the main river," I said, peering down at the water rushing past below the bank where we were standing. "At least I hope so! It's definitely not appropriate for rafting in this spot."

By now the moon was rising, making it a little easier to see. The tributary was moving even faster than the main river. It had eaten out a narrow, twisting ravine studded with sharp-looking rocks.

"It's not really appropriate for crossing on foot, either," Bess said. "I hope whoever we're following realizes that."

"What if this person is just trying to get us lost out here?" George flapped her hands at some random bugs buzzing around her head. "It could take weeks to find us."

I had to admit the thought had occurred to me. But I wasn't willing to give up yet. Tilting my head, I listened for another signal from our mysterious caller.

I didn't hear any more loon calls. But I did hear something else. A sort of hollow gurgling sound.

"Listen," I said. "Do you guys hear that?" I started walking along the riverbank toward the source of the sound.

"Sounds like water to me," George said with a shrug. "Probably just another stream breaking off or something."

But Bess let out a gasp. "Look over there!" she cried, pointing.

I followed her finger to a huge metal pipe jutting out of the cut-out bank on the far side of the tributary. Vines hung down over there, mostly obscuring it. But it looked as if someone had recently hacked away some of the foliage to make the pipe more visible.

George peered across at it. "What's that all about?" she asked, staring at the liquid pouring out of it.

"I don't know," I began. "I wonder if . . ."

My voice trailed off as a breeze wafted through the

jungle. It carried a smell with it from the direction of that pipe. And not a pleasant one.

"Ugh!" Bess cried, covering her nose. "Gross. Is that? . . ."

"Human waste," I said grimly, suddenly guessing what this little midnight trek was all about. "Unless I miss my guess, that's got to be unfiltered human waste."

"Did you tell Cristobal about what we saw last night?" Bess whispered to me as I sat down to breakfast the next morning.

I glanced quickly around the dining room. Nearby, Kat was regaling the others with her usual Hollywood tales as she fed Pretty Boy pieces of bacon. I'd already noted that the little dog was even more dressed up than usual today. He was wrapped in a tiny grass skirt and a bikini top that appeared to be made of walnuts. A jaunty straw sun hat finished off the outfit.

"I tried," I replied to my friends. "He promised he'd look into it. But he seemed to think I must have dreamed the whole thing." I rolled my eyes as I recalled the resort owner's reaction, which had pretty much amounted to a "there, there" and a pat on the head.

George shook her head. "I just wish I'd been able to trace where that call came from," she muttered. "For such a state-of-the-art place, the phone technology here is awfully backward. . . ."

We had to stop talking about the case when Hildy and Robin arrived and came over to sit with us. After that, we spent the meal discussing what the resort might have planned for our last two full days there.

Just as breakfast ended, the Green Solutions camera crew arrived. It consisted of a director, an assistant director, and half a dozen camera operators and other techs.

Kat and Deirdre immediately rushed over to introduce themselves. The next few minutes were pretty chaotic as the two of them talked the director's ear off, the crew started setting up equipment, and Cristobal did his best to oversee the whole scene. Despite looking a bit overwhelmed by all the action, Pretty Boy managed not to bite anyone, at least while I was watching. I couldn't help wondering if Cristobal had called ahead to warn the crew about him.

I also noticed that Poppy was hovering around Kat and Deirdre. Wandering a bit closer, I heard her chattering at them about clothes, accessories, makeup, that sort of thing. That explained it. The cousins must have commandeered her to advise them on fashion, given her position with a world-famous fashion magazine. Fortunately, Poppy seemed happy to help out. In fact, she looked happier than I'd seen her in days.

Bess noticed too. "Think Poppy's in such a good mood because she's doing her thing, or is it because Adam isn't around?" she murmured with a raised eyebrow.

"Could be either one," I whispered back. "Maybe both."

As I glanced around the lobby, I noted that Adam was just about the only one missing. Enrique and the rest of the hospitality staff were peeking out from the kitchen. Alicia was bustling around rearranging the flower arrangements while keeping one eye on the action. The other guests were hanging out in the lobby watching openly. Among them were Robin and her mother.

"Ah, and who *do* we have here?" exclaimed the director, a tall man who had introduced himself as Harvey. He rushed over to Robin. "What's your name, sweetheart?"

"Robin," she replied shyly.

He chucked her under the chin. "You're adorable!" he cried. "We have to get you into some of the shots. Should work splendidly with our 'green for the future' theme. What do you say, darling?"

After a consult with Hildy it was agreed that Robin would be featured in the very first bit they shot.

Kat and Deirdre didn't seem too pleased with that. I guess Pretty Boy wasn't either, because when Kat set him down for a second, he made a break for it, racing toward the nearest exit.

"I know, I know, baby," Kat muttered as she hurried after him. "This isn't how it's supposed to go. Everyone always says not to work with kids or animals."

She grabbed the little dog. He yapped excitedly and chomped down on her finger.

"Ow!" Kat yelped. Yanking her finger out of Pretty Boy's tiny jaws, she tucked him under one arm and rushed back to the others.

George was grinning as she watched the whole scene. "Now, *that's* entertainment," she commented.

"So's the circus," Bess said wryly. "But I've never been much of a fan of that, either. Should we get out of here?"

I nodded. "Maybe while everyone's distracted, we can snoop around the rest of the place a little."

The three of us headed for the door. I was pretty sure nobody even noticed our departure. Soon we were emerging into the garden area behind the dining room.

Thunk! I heard a strange sound from somewhere nearby.

Looking in the direction of the sound, I let out a

gasp. There was someone digging around in one of the trash Dumpsters right outside the kitchen door a few yards away. And when that someone straightened up and glanced around, I recognized her immediately.

It was the crazy-eyed, wild-haired blond woman we'd seen in town the evening before!

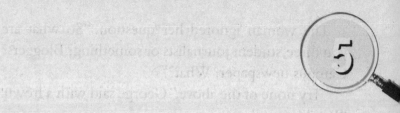

AT FACE VALUE

"**H**ey!" I blurted out, hurrying toward her. "What are you doing?"

The woman jumped and spun around, looking startled. She was dressed in Bermuda shorts and an ANIMALS ARE PEOPLE TOO T-shirt, both studded with environmentally themed pins.

Her surprise passed quickly, her watery blue eyes narrowing. "I know you," she said, pointing a pudgy finger at each of us in turn. "You were in town last night with the Casa Verde crew. Are you staying here?"

"That's right," Bess said. "But who are you, and what are you doing here?"

The woman ignored her question. "So what are you three, student journalists or something? Bloggers? Campus newspaper? What?"

"Try none of the above," George said with a frown. "But listen—"

Once again, the woman plowed ahead. "It doesn't matter," she said, wiping some limp lettuce off one hand onto her shorts. "Listen, whoever you are, you look like nice girls. I'm sure you're in favor of green causes. You've got to help me expose this place to the outside world!"

"You mean Casa Verde?" I spoke up. "Expose it as what?"

"As an environmental disaster!" The woman threw her hands up over her head, her round cheeks practically quivering with distress. "It claims to be green, but some of us know better. This press week thing is the perfect chance to expose that before the general public is fooled."

My mind immediately jumped to that sewer pipe, then to the whispery female voice on the phone, and finally to all the notes that had appeared around Casa Verde during our stay. We'd thought Juliana had left the notes. Could we have been wrong about that?

"What are you saying?" I asked the woman, taking a step closer. "Have you seen problems here at Casa Verde? You know—by looking deeper?"

The woman looked confused. "What do you mean? All I know is that the truth is all over the Internet. The greenie blogs are on fire with it! That's why I had to come right away. I just arrived in San Isidro yesterday afternoon from my home over on the Caribbean coast."

George furrowed her brow. "You mean, you live in Costa Rica?" she said. "But you read about Casa Verde on the Net? Who are you, anyway?"

"Oh!" The woman let out a giggle. "Sorry, where are my manners? I just get so impassioned over this stuff. . . . Anyway, my name's Phyllis. Phyllis Pitt. I'm a warrior for planet Earth."

"I see," Bess said politely as she shook the woman's hand, though it was clear that she didn't.

"That's why I moved to Costa Rica," Phyllis went on as she shook my hand as well. "I wanted to support the country's environmental policies and do whatever I can to help."

George looked dismayed as Phyllis stuck out her hand to her next. I guessed George was thinking about that gooey lettuce Phyllis had just wiped off it. But she shook her hand anyway. "So what's all this about Casa Verde not being green?" George asked.

Phyllis's face darkened as she glanced at the trash Dumpsters. "I told you, everyone's chatting about it.

I came up here to protest as soon as I arrived in the area yesterday."

Aha! That explained at least one thing—why the resort employees had recognized her and called her a troublemaker. I figured Phyllis's protest must have taken place while most of us had been off snorkeling the day before.

"The earth-hating scoundrels here chased me off," Phyllis went on with another grim look around. "But my cause is righteous, so I won't be frightened away by their strong-arm tactics. I'm determined to expose the wrongdoings here."

"By digging through the trash?" George said dubiously.

"Actually, that sort of makes sense," Bess put in before Phyllis could respond. "If this place isn't recycling their waste properly, it might mean there are other problems." She shot me a look, and I guessed she was thinking about that pipe, too.

"You see?" Phyllis sang out, clasping her hands and looking delighted. "I knew you were nice girls! I'm a very good judge of character. So will you help me?"

I shrugged. "Might as well take a look," I said. "If only to put those Internet rumors to rest."

"But I don't get why there are rumors to start with," George said. "I did some online research myself before we came here, remember? Casa Verde isn't just a local project. Its whole design and creation were supervised by Green Solutions. And I didn't find anything negative about them."

Phyllis clucked sympathetically. "It's lovely that you're so innocent, dear," she told George. "But you need to figure out how to use the Web to get more reliable information. You might not know enough about where to look for the truth."

"What?" George exclaimed, sounding outraged.

I hid a smile as I shot Bess a look. If there was one thing that got George riled up, it was someone questioning her tech skills.

Phyllis didn't seem to notice. "Besides," she went on, "it's only in the past week or so that brave souls have started spreading the truth."

"There you go, George," Bess said. "I'm sure you wouldn't be so, you know, *innocent* if you hadn't been without your laptop all week."

"Whatever," George muttered, still looking annoyed.

"Come on," I said. I wasn't sure if there was anything to Phyllis's rants, but if it was a dead end, I didn't want to waste too much time. We didn't have long to solve this thing as it was. "Let's go ahead and check out these trash containers."

Soon all four of us were climbing up and peering into the line of metal containers behind the kitchen.

It turned out that the one Phyllis had been digging through contained only organic kitchen waste—Bess spotted a stenciled sign on the side indicating it was destined for composting elsewhere on the property. Various other bins held plastics, papers, and so on. The smallest bin of all was labeled NONRECYCLABLES and was nearly empty.

"There." Bess stepped back from the final container, brushing off her hands. "Looks like everything's in order. Actually, I'm impressed by how thoroughly they separate the trash here."

Phyllis frowned. "Separating garbage is the easy part," she said, sounding sort of disappointed. "It doesn't mean they aren't ravaging the earth in tons of other ways."

My friends and I exchanged looks. Phyllis seemed to mean well. But she also came across as pretty fanatical—verging on loony, actually.

She glanced at us and narrowed her eyes, seeming to note our skeptical expressions. "I thought journalists were supposed to be interested in digging for stories," she snapped. "Not just accepting stuff at face value!"

With that, she turned and stomped off, disappearing around the corner of the building. I don't think any of us were sorry to see her go.

"What a nut," George declared, kicking aside a tin

can that had fallen out of one of the bins during our search.

I bit my lip. "Yeah," I agreed. "But did you hear what she said? About digging for stories? Remind you of anything?"

Bess's eyes widened. "Digging," she echoed. "Like, digging deeper?"

"Wait, are you two saying you think our new pal Phyllis could've written all those notes?" George said. "I thought we already decided that was Juliana."

"We did, at least until another note turned up on that turtle," Bess reminded her. "What if Phyllis has been doing it all along?"

"But she said she only arrived in this area yesterday," I said. "If she's been off halfway across the country until then, there's really no way she could have left those notes, or dognapped Pretty Boy, or the rest of it."

George shrugged. "That's what she claims, anyway. If I can get to a computer, I'll try to check out her story about when she got here."

"Good idea," Bess said. "Because aside from the timing, she's kind of looking like a good suspect." She grinned. "Though it's hard to imagine her dragging that stuffed turtle around. . . ."

We were all still chuckling at that image when we heard voices nearby. A moment later, the film crew came hurrying around the corner. Deirdre, Kat, and Pretty Boy were with them, along with Cristobal.

"Here you go, gentlemen," Cristobal announced, sweeping a hand in the direction of the trash bins. "Our state-of-the-art recycling station."

He went on to describe how the resort's recycling program worked, but I wasn't focused on that. I couldn't help wondering—if Cristobal knew the crew was planning to shoot some footage of this area, could he have cleaned it up just for show? What if Phyllis was right, and Casa Verde wasn't this "green" when the cameras weren't around?

She might come across as a little nutty, but maybe she has a point, I mused, feeling troubled. *Like journalists, detectives shouldn't take things at face value. . . .*

"So what do you think we should do next?" George asked as we wandered along an orchid-lined path a few minutes later.

I sighed. "I'm not sure," I admitted. "I guess we should get in touch with Juliana again. Even with her alibi for the turtle thing, she's still our strongest suspect."

We rounded a curve in the trail. That brought us within sight of a little cluster of bamboo huts. From earlier explorations I knew this was the groundskeeping and animal care complex. Alicia and Sara shared an office in the largest building, which also contained a greenhouse, a small laboratory, and a well-stocked medical facility for treating injured animals from the reserve. A second building was a combination office and tool room for the grounds staff. There was also a small library of books and videos in one of the smaller huts. The others were supply and equipment sheds. A larger machine shed for the trucks, tractors, and other heavy equipment stood off to one side.

At the moment, Sara was raking the dirt-and-gravel yard in front of the vet building. She spun around when we stepped into view.

"Oh!" she exclaimed. "You guys scared me."

"Sorry." I smiled at her. "We're just taking a walk. What are you up to?"

"Nothing." She clutched the rake handle with both hands. "I mean, just cleaning up. Alicia got the four-wheeler stuck in the mud here the other day after it rained, and I wanted to fix the ruts."

Bess stepped forward, peering at some faint tire tracks in the dirt. "Those marks don't look like they were made by a four-wheeler," she commented. "More like a full-size truck."

Did I mention Bess is a total gearhead? You wouldn't know it by looking at her frilly dresses and flawless makeup, but she's a whiz with cars and anything mechanical.

Sara looked a little surprised. "You're right," she agreed. "Um, we tried to flatten out the ruts with the truck first. But that just made things worse." She glanced at her watch. "Oops! I need to go!" she exclaimed. "I just realized I'm late. Sorry . . ."

She dropped her rake, then rushed off. George watched her go, looking confused.

"Okay, that was weird," she said when Sara was out of earshot.

"I have to admit, Sara was kind of acting like someone with something to hide," I said. "But we already know she's kind of shy. I don't think she's that comfortable talking to people most of the time. Maybe that's why she wanted to get away."

"Or maybe she's covering for Alicia," Bess suggested. "What if Alicia made those ruts transporting that sea turtle? Sara could be trying to protect her boss—maybe without even knowing what she was really doing."

"I guess it's possible," I said dubiously. "But Alicia was with us all day yesterday, remember? She couldn't have planted that turtle, even with all the trucks in the world at her disposal."

George nodded. "Well, what about Sara herself? Think she could have done it? She *is* pretty close to Juliana's age—what if she's the accomplice we've been speculating about?"

"It's possible," I said. "I still think we need to talk to Juliana about all this. Maybe I can get her to tell me what's really going on."

I remembered that there was a guest phone in one of the cabanas near the pool. We hurried back there. Luckily, the pool area was deserted.

Juliana picked up her cell phone right away. "Nancy!" she said when she heard it was me. She sounded surprised but not too upset to hear from me. It seemed she wasn't the type to hold a grudge. "How are you?"

"I'm fine," I said. "I just wanted to check in and see if you heard about all the excitement here yesterday."

"You mean the crazy protest lady?" Juliana chuckled. "*Sí*, my papa told me he had to help banish her from Casa Verde."

"Did he tell you about the sea turtle?"

"Sea turtle? What do you mean?"

She sounded sincerely confused, though I knew she could be faking that. After all, she'd done a pretty convincing job of faking innocence when we'd found Pretty Boy in her room.

I told her about the turtle incident. *"Dios mio!"* she exclaimed. "That is terrible. Sea turtles are endangered. It is not funny even to play a prank about such a thing."

"That's not all," I went on. "Last night my friends and I found something in the jungle. A big pipe pouring human waste directly into the river. And we're pretty sure it's coming from right here at Casa Verde. Have you seen anything like that around here?"

"A pipe? No, of course not. I've seen nothing like that."

Was it my imagination? Or did her voice sound funny now?

Before I could ask her anything else, the film crew suddenly popped into view at the edge of the pool area. As usual, Deirdre and Kat were with them. So was Poppy.

I told Juliana I had to go and hung up. When I turned around, George was grinning.

"Check it out," she said in a low voice. "Looks like Deirdre's been demoted from costar to animal wrangler."

Indeed, Deirdre seemed to have been relegated to holding Pretty Boy while her cousin prepared for her big scene. Poppy was fluttering around Kat, touching up her makeup, fluffing her hair, and adjusting the straps on her glamorous-looking silver and black bikini.

"Excuse me, miss!" one of the crew members said, shuffling Deirdre and Pretty Boy even farther away from the action. "Step back, please. We need to get that umbrella out of the way."

I glanced over at the waterfall at the far end of the pool. One of the shade umbrellas that normally stood over the poolside tables appeared to have blown over there and caught on one of the rocks or something, so that it almost completely obscured the view of the picturesque waterfall.

"That's right," the assistant director said, sounding irritated. He was a short, somewhat stocky man with a perpetual frown. He glared at the waterfall. "Who put that thing there, anyway? I was told the pool would be ready for this shot! Time is money, people. . . ."

Harvey, the main director, only rolled his eyes. "Relax, Michaels," he told the other man. "We'll have it out of the way in a moment."

"Ow!" Deirdre shrieked, suddenly jerking her hand away from Pretty Boy's mouth. "Quit it, you little jerk!"

She set the dog down. He promptly lifted one hind leg over her foot, eliciting another shriek of horror.

"Are you kidding me?" she yelled. "These sandals weren't cheap, you know!"

"Should we get while the getting's good?" Bess asked as we watched.

"No way!" George exclaimed. "I don't want to miss a second of this."

I was about to remind her how little time we had left at Casa Verde. But before I could, there was a shout from the far end of the pool. Glancing over there, I saw that the crew member had just wrestled the umbrella out of the way.

That left us all with a clear view of the waterfall— and the graffiti that someone had scrawled across the rock face in bold black letters:

STOP WASTING TIME IN THE SHALLOW END. LOOK DEEPER BEFORE TIME RUNS OUT!

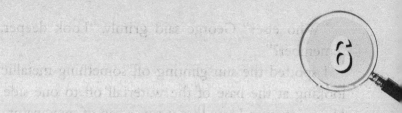

ZIPPING ALONG

There was a moment of chaos as everyone got a good look at the message on the waterfall. Someone ran to get Cristobal. Kat started whining about her shot being ruined. Harvey, sounding a little frustrated, ordered the assistant director to go scout a new location so they wouldn't waste the daylight.

"Come on," I said to my friends. "Let's go check it out."

"Do you think whoever wrote those notes did this, too?" Bess asked as we scooted toward the waterfall.

"Who else?" George said grimly. "Look deeper, remember?"

I spotted the sun glinting off something metallic looking at the base of the waterfall off to one side. Hurrying over, I saw that it was a can of spray paint.

"Sloppy work," I said with satisfaction. "Unless the culprit was wearing gloves, this should tell us something."

"What's going on out here?"

I turned and saw Cristobal rushing into view. Enrique was right behind him. Both brothers looked confused and anxious.

Kat and Deirdre started ranting about having their lives ruined or whatever. I wasn't paying much attention to them, and neither was Harvey.

"This is right in the middle of our shot," he complained to the Arrojo brothers, stabbing one finger toward the waterfall.

Cristobal glanced over, his face blanching as he read the graffiti. He moved closer for a better look.

"Check it out," I called to him as he approached, pointing to the spray paint can. "If you take this to the police, maybe they can—"

"The police? Nonsense." Cristobal swooped forward, grabbing the can before I could protest. He glared at it, then tossed it into a nearby wastebasket. "I won't let this vandal ruin the reputation of Casa Verde!"

Enrique looked kind of tense. "Maybe we should just talk to the police," he said in his quieter voice. "If things keep on this way ..."

"Nonsense!" Cristobal snapped again. He glowered at his brother. "We will take care of it ourselves."

Enrique narrowed his eyes, looking as if he were about to say something. But he merely pursed his lips tightly, shaking his head as he turned away from his brother.

Yikes! You could practically cut the tension with a knife. Were they just upset about this latest incident? Or was there something else going on? I flashed back to that witnessed—but not heard—face-off by this very same pool the night before. What had they been arguing about?

"Listen, Cristobal," Harvey said. "We have a schedule here, and if we can't get the footage we need ..."

"Yes, yes, of course." Cristobal was clearly struggling to regain his usual good cheer. "We'll find a way to make it work. At Casa Verde we pride ourselves on coming up with creative solutions—just like all of you at Green Solutions, hmm?"

"I wouldn't know about that." Harvey sounded kind of sour. "I'm just a freelancer on this project. You'll have to talk to Michaels about that sort of synergy garbage."

"Never mind. Enrique, why don't you see if Harvey and his people would like a beverage?" Cristobal noticed that my friends and I were still watching, along with the irritated-looking Deirdre and Kat. "As for you, ladies, you'll need to hurry—the bus will be departing for the zip line tour in just a short while."

Oops. I'd almost forgotten about today's scheduled activity. All the guests were supposed to visit a facility that allowed people to glide through the rain forest canopy on a gravity-powered cable ride.

"Zip line?" Kat made a face. "Think we'll give that a pass. We're busy starring in your ads, remember?"

Harvey's cranky expression faded. "Zip-lining, eh? Sounds exciting. Mind if we tag along and get some footage?"

"Not at all!" Cristobal looked relieved. "That's an excellent idea. Now, hurry, everyone—the bus leaves in twenty minutes!"

"Zip-lining sounds fun, but I kind of wish we didn't have to go," I murmured to my friends as we settled ourselves on the Casa Verde bus twenty minutes later. "We're running out of time if we want to figure out what's really going on around here."

"I know." George grinned sheepishly. "But I have to admit, zip-lining sounds like a blast!"

Bess nodded. "I'm looking forward to it too," she said. "It's supposed to be one of the best, most low-impact ways to view the rain forest." She scanned the crowded bus and lowered her voice. "Besides, some of our suspects are here, right?"

She had a point. Both Poppy and Adam were sharing a seat near the back of the bus, though they didn't appear to be speaking to each other. Sarene was present as well. I guessed even she couldn't find anything to complain about when it came to today's activity.

Just then Enrique appeared at the front of the bus. He cleared his throat as he glanced at Pedro, who was in the driver's seat as usual.

"Everyone on board?" Enrique asked the driver.

"What are you doing here?" Frankie called out from her seat beside Sarene. "Where's Cristobal?"

"My brother was called away at the last moment," Enrique replied with a slight frown. "I shall accompany you in his place."

He didn't sound too happy about that. I couldn't help wondering about the substitution. While gregarious Cristobal seemed to enjoy hanging out with us guests, Enrique obviously wasn't nearly as comfortable with that sort of public role, preferring to stay mostly behind the scenes in the kitchen.

George seemed to be thinking the same thing.

"I'm guessing Alicia is going to have to do most of the talking today," she whispered.

Bess nodded, looking over at the seat right behind Pedro. The biologist and her assistant were sitting there. "Maybe Sara, too," she suggested. "She did an awfully good job at the presentation last night."

"Here we are!" Kat trilled, bouncing onto the bus behind Enrique. "Sorry we're late! Pretty Boy wanted to change clothes so he'd be dressed for the occasion."

She giggled and held up the dog. He glared at all of us from beneath the brim of a feathered hat. The rest of him was encased in what appeared to be an iridescent spandex catsuit. He looked totally ridiculous—though, of course, that was nothing new. Kat seemed to have a never-ending supply of outfits for him.

Deirdre was right behind her cousin. "Hurry up," she said, giving her a poke.

I couldn't help noticing that she, too, had changed clothes in the last twenty minutes. She was wearing a form-fitting halter top and shorts, along with a pair of sparkly high-heeled sandals.

"Think she's hoping that getup will grab her more camera time?" George whispered.

I glanced at the camera crew. Despite his enthusiasm about the zip-lining, Harvey wasn't there. But he'd

sent the assistant director, along with a couple of the camera operators.

"Probably," I agreed quietly. "I don't think she's happy that Kat is grabbing most of the attention."

By now Kat was flouncing down the bus aisle to the only remaining seat. "Don't worry, baby," she said to Pretty Boy. "I'm sure one of these nice cameramen will keep an eye on you while Mommy is zip-lining. We wouldn't want to leave you with just *anyone*, you know. Not after what happened last time." She shot a disapproving look toward Pedro.

"You mean you're not going to let Pretty Boy go zip-lining with you, Kat?" Hildy spoke up.

I was almost sure she was joking around. But Kat took the question seriously.

"Oh no," she replied, hugging Pretty Boy. "My baby is afraid of heights."

Deirdre rolled her eyes as she flopped down into the seat beside her cousin. "More like *you're* afraid of heights," she told her.

The bus started up at that moment, distracting everybody. Robin let out a little cheer, and most of the others laughed and joined in. As Pedro steered down the drive, Alicia stood up and faced the rest of us.

"Okay, everyone," she said cheerfully. "Let's talk about some of what we're going to see today. . . ."

When we arrived at the zip line place, the employees there started by giving us a tour of the facilities and showing us the zip lines. The lines were actually thick cables strung high up over the canopy, beginning at several tall platforms at the top of a hill and ending at another platform near the bottom. The employees explained that there was also a steam-powered trolley to return riders back up to the starting point once they landed.

"Awesome!" Adam exclaimed, cracking his knuckles as he peered up at one of the platforms. "I can't wait to try it out. Can I go first?"

"Not so fast," Alicia said with a chuckle as Poppy rolled her eyes. "We have a few things to take care of first. Let's go in out of the sun for a moment and get started."

As we all trooped after her toward a large bamboo hut, the assistant director ordered the crew to stay outside with him to get some establishing shots. Kat and Deirdre insisted on joining them, obviously hoping for some extra screen time. But Alicia, Enrique, and the zip line employees politely shooed them inside with the rest of us.

The hut was airy and pleasant, with ceiling fans keeping most of the bugs away despite the lack of screens on the windows. We all sat down at a couple of long wooden tables. First we all signed some releases, and after that, Sara started passing out printouts detailing the plants, animals, and birds we might see in this part of the forest.

"At first it might be hard to concentrate while you're getting used to hanging so high up in the air," Alicia told us as we all looked over the information. "But the zip line is very safe, so you don't have to worry. I hope you'll be able to look around and enjoy the unique view."

As she walked us through the handouts, I was only half listening. Instead my mind drifted back to the case as my gaze wandered from one face to another. Enrique, Poppy, Adam, Sarene, Alicia, Sara. Bess had been right—most of our suspects were right there in the room. True, Juliana and Cristobal were missing, and so was Phyllis. But we already knew Juliana couldn't be working alone and that Phyllis probably hadn't been around for most of the incidents. And Cristobal had always been a weak suspect at best.

I guess we'll just have to wait and see if we find anything new and disturbing when we return to Casa Verde, I thought. *If we do, we'll be able to cross a few more people off the list.*

By the time I tuned back in, Alicia was just wrapping up her talk. She glanced at a zip line employee who had just appeared holding a tray of sodas.

Alicia smiled and waved him forward. "And now before we get started, the lovely people here will be serving us a traditional Costa Rican lunch."

"Are you sure you want us to eat before we go up there?" Deirdre spoke up with a smirk. "Kat's afraid of heights—it might be better if she tried this sort of thing when her stomach's empty."

Kat shot her an annoyed look. "I don't know what you're talking about. It's Pretty Boy who's afraid of heights, not me."

Out of the corner of my eye I noticed movement near the back of the group. Glancing that way, I was just in time to see Poppy slipping out the door. Where could she be going at a time like this? I had no idea, but I intended to find out.

"Be right back," I murmured to George beside me.

I got up and hurried after Poppy. Outside I was just in time to see her disappear into the restroom, which was located in a separate building.

Oh well, I thought sheepishly. *Not so mysterious after all.*

I turned to head back into the main hut. As I did, a flash of movement caught my eye. Someone was hurrying around the edge of the building, heading into the jungle.

"Hey," I blurted out. "Who's there?"

The figure darted away, disappearing from view. I raced after it, but by the time I rounded the corner myself, there was no one in sight.

I just stood there for a moment listening to distant monkey calls and thinking about what I'd just witnessed. The encounter had been so fast that I'd barely gotten a look at the figure. All I'd seen was a person a little below average height and a little above average weight, dressed in lightweight khaki slacks, a white T-shirt, and a large straw hat that completely covered his or her hair. The outfit had been pretty much identical to what several members of our group were wearing, including Hildy, Frankie, the entire film crew, and even Bess, though the mystery figure had been stockier than any of them except Mr. Michaels and one of the cameramen. I wasn't even sure whether it had been a man or a woman.

Could it have been someone looking for trouble? I wondered. *Maybe even Phyllis? I think that person was about the right size and shape. . . .*

"Excuse me, *señorita*," a polite voice broke my thoughts. "Will you please rejoin the group inside?"

It was a member of the zip line staff. I blinked at him. "Oh, sorry," I said. "I was only, um, looking around."

I allowed him to guide me back around the corner. Enrique had just emerged and was standing outside fiddling with his cell phone. He looked surprised to see me.

"Nancy," he said. "What are you doing out here? They are serving lunch inside."

I couldn't help noticing that he sounded a little frazzled. Was that just a result of having to come along with us in his brother's place, or could there be something else going on?

Either way, it seemed I wasn't going to find out anything more right now. I headed inside to eat.

Kat pulled out a compact and checked her makeup. "I'm ready," she called out, snapping the compact shut again. "Should I go first?"

"If you like, yes, of course," the head zip line employee said. "This way, please."

Kat glanced over to make sure one of the cameramen was filming her. Then she bent down to scoop up Pretty Boy, who was sitting quietly for once in the shade of a large hibiscus.

"Don't worry, baby," she crooned. "Mommy will be back soon! The nice men will take care of you while I'm gone."

She hurried over and shoved the little dog toward the assistant director, Mr. Michaels, who was on his cell phone nearby. Pretty Boy yapped and tried to bite him.

Mr. Michaels dodged just in time, hanging up his phone and tucking it back into the pocket of his khakis. "All right, people," he called out. "Let's get started. You go first, Miss."

He turned and pointed at . . . me?

"You want me to go first?" I said in surprise.

"Her?" Kat added, freezing in place with Pretty Boy still dangling from her outstretched hands. "But *I* was going to go first! After all, I'm the one who's supposed to be featured in this ad!"

"That's right." The assistant director gestured vaguely toward the cameras. "I want to test the camera angles on someone else first."

"Oh." Kat looked mollified. "All right. That makes sense—come to think of it, they do that sort of thing on all the big pictures I've worked on." She stepped back into the shade with Pretty Boy.

"How about me taking the first shot at this, then?" Adam stepped forward, flexing his biceps. "I know they say ladies first, but in this case I think what you need is a man."

"Thank you, but no," Mr. Michaels said firmly. "This young lady is just right to test our lighting and such properly. If you please, Miss Drew?"

"Um, okay." I was looking forward to the zip line,

so I wasn't going to argue. Besides, going first might give me more time to question some of my suspects afterward. Plus, the earlier I went, the more likely I might spot that mysterious Phyllis-like figure in the jungle below. . . .

Soon I was standing atop the thirty-foot platform, outfitted in a zip line harness. One of the employees hooked me to the line.

"Ready?" he asked.

I nodded and stepped forward. "Wheeee!" I called out as my feet left the platform and I felt myself gliding through the air.

But my stomach lurched as the line jerked roughly. Weird. Zip-lining had always looked like it would feel smooth, sort of like flying. But as I spun downward toward the edge of the flat area where the huts and platforms were located, the line jerked again and again.

Below, I heard people shouting. But I didn't pay attention to that. I was focused on hanging on. By now I was pretty sure something was wrong.

A moment later, the line jerked again, harder this time. Then it snapped, and I felt myself flung free into thin air. I was falling . . . falling . . .

DEEPER AND DEEPER

"It's lucky the line broke before you passed the drop-off into the canopy," Bess said, her voice shaking.

I just nodded. She and George—and many of the others—had said the same thing multiple times in the ten minutes since my fall. And they were right. Five seconds later, and I wouldn't have been sitting there with nothing worse than a few scratches and bruises. I'd tumbled down only about fifteen feet, with a leafy palm tree and a small, muddy pond softening my fall.

"Are you sure you wouldn't like to leave now?"

Enrique asked, his eyes wide and his voice frantic. I'd never seen him so upset, not even during the whole Juliana situation.

"No, I'm fine," I insisted again. "I don't want to ruin everyone else's fun."

I glanced around, wondering just how much fun the others were having. Kat had been hysterical since the incident, babbling "It could have been me!" over and over again while clutching Pretty Boy to her chest. Young Robin looked shaken and pale, while her mother, Hildy, was keeping a baleful eye on the video cameras, which she'd ordered shut off immediately after my fall. Frankie was insisting to anyone who would listen that she would use her investigative journalism skills to get to the bottom of this. The zip line people were horrified, chattering incessantly at one another in Spanish in between profuse apologies to all of us in English, with the manager offering me free zip line passes for life.

In the midst of all this, Poppy wandered up to the group. I realized I hadn't seen her since following her out to the restroom earlier; I wasn't even sure whether she'd ever come back inside to eat lunch or not.

"What's going on?" she asked, pushing her fashionably oversize sunglasses farther up her nose.

Adam hurried over. "You missed all the action,

babe," he said, putting a protective arm around her. "There was a malfunction and Nancy took a tumble."

Poppy shook off his arm. "She did? What happened?"

Several voices spoke up at once, eagerly describing the accident. Meanwhile, George leaned toward me.

"Are you sure you don't want to head back to the resort, Nance?" she asked quietly. "We might all be better off. What if the same thing happens again?"

"I doubt it will," I said, doing my best to shake off the last of my shock. "This zip line place has the best safety record in Costa Rica, remember? Alicia mentioned that on the drive over. What are the odds the line would break while we were here—especially right after I saw someone lurking around out there near the base of the platforms?"

"What?" Bess exclaimed softly. "Who was lurking?"

Looking around to make sure no one else was paying attention, I quickly filled them in on that mysterious figure. George let out a gasp.

"Do you think it could have been Phyllis?" she asked.

I shrugged. "Yeah," I said. "But I'm really not sure at all. The point is, whoever it was could've sneaked out and messed with the equipment while all of us were inside."

"Or anyone from the group could have done

it," Bess pointed out. "I think just about everybody left the dining room at some point during lunch, either to use the bathroom or get more bug spray or whatever."

The same thought had already occurred to me. I surveyed the group, trying to gauge the reactions of our various suspects. Sarene wasn't reacting much; if anything, she looked a little bored. Alicia and Sara looked shocked and confused just like everyone else. Adam was one of the people telling his girlfriend what had happened; he seemed worked up and almost excited about the whole situation. It was impossible to read Poppy's expression behind her dark glasses, but she was being very quiet since asking her question.

"So who looks suspicious to you guys?" I murmured to my friends.

George shrugged. "Adam, maybe? He seems to be enjoying this a little too much."

"He always acts like that, though, doesn't he?" Bess said.

I sighed, wishing I'd tried harder to follow that mysterious figure into the jungle. Without knowing who it had been, it was difficult, if not impossible, to guess who might have sabotaged that zip line.

Just then Enrique hurried back over. "If you are sure you really do not wish to depart . . . ," he began, gazing at me with concern.

"I'm sure," I said firmly, convinced of that now more than ever. The zip line employees were already swarming around the other platforms, checking and rechecking the equipment, which made me feel pretty confident that there wouldn't be a repeat. In which case, I realized, this might be my last good opportunity to break this case.

Enrique nodded, still looking uncertain. "All right," he said. "Then *por favor*, just relax here in the shade and try to recover your wits."

"Thanks."

I sat there, sipping on the drink Pedro had brought me and watching the scene. Bess and George stayed with me, and the others wandered over now and then to check on me. Within a few minutes the zip line manager spoke up, assuring us all that the other lines were in perfect working order. He even sent one of the employees up to demonstrate. The young man jumped off the platform and zipped down the line without a hitch, eventually disappearing from our sight into the canopy far below. A few minutes later, he radioed up to his boss to let him know he'd landed safely.

"You see? It is working fine now," the manager said. "I do hope you will all enjoy the rest of your time here. And I can assure you that this visit is free for all of you today."

Adam pumped his fist and let out a little cheer. Poppy shot him a look of disgust, while Hildy and Sarene rolled their eyes. The others just ignored him.

"Are you sure it's safe?" Kat called out, her voice shaking.

"Quite sure," the manager assured her.

"But nobody has to go if they do not feel comfortable," Enrique added.

"That's right," the assistant director spoke up. "We can just get some footage of the employees doing the zip line if you don't want to do it, Kat."

Kat gulped. I could almost see the struggle playing out on her face—torn between the fear of dying and the fear of not being prominently featured in the ad. Finally the second fear won, just as I would have predicted.

"No, I'm okay," she said, still sounding nervous. "The show must go on, right?"

Adam stepped forward. "Want me to go first, Kat?" he offered eagerly. "You know—test it out, make sure it's safe."

"No, thanks." Kat handed Pretty Boy to Deirdre and hurried forward, pushing past him. "Let's just get this over with. I'm ready."

We could all see Kat shaking, even way up atop the platform, as the employees strapped her in. And the first scream when she jumped off sounded like she was pretty terrified. But the line held, and she zipped away smoothly with the cameras filming the whole thing.

After that, the others seemed much more willing to give it a try. Adam went next, followed by Deirdre, Frankie, Robin, and George.

"Guess that means I'm on deck," Bess said, standing up and brushing off her shorts as Hildy started climbing the platform. "Will you be okay until I get back?"

"I'm fine. Go on and have fun." As Bess hurried off, I noticed Poppy wandering over to stand in the shade nearby. "Are you going to take a turn?" I called to her, trying to sound friendly.

She stepped toward me. "I'm not sure," she admitted. The dark glasses still hid her expression, but her voice belied her nervousness. "After what happened to you . . ."

I just nodded, not really interested in talking about zip-lining. Once I'd realized that Poppy might not have rejoined us for lunch earlier, I couldn't stop wondering what she'd been doing for so long. Had she really spent the whole time in the bathroom? Or could she have sneaked out—maybe to mess with that zip line? For all I knew, that other mystery figure was a red herring, and the true culprit was someone from our group.

"I noticed you left for a while during lunch," I said, doing my best to keep my voice casual and concerned. "I hope your stomach wasn't bothering you or something."

"What?" Poppy had turned to watch Bess start the climb up the platform. But now she jerked her head toward me again. "Um, you did? I mean, yes. I wasn't feeling too well." She let out a short laugh. "Sorry, it's just a little embarrassing."

I nodded, trying to look sympathetic. But my mind was racing. Poppy definitely seemed nervous. Was it really embarrassment, or was she hiding something?

We both turned to watch Bess leap off the platform and glide through the air overhead. As Sarene stepped forward for her turn, I turned my attention back to Poppy.

But before I could figure out how to continue my questioning, a voice shouted her name. It was Adam. He'd just returned from his glide down the mountainside.

"That was awesome!" he exclaimed, bolting over to us. "You've got to try it, babe. What a rush!"

"I don't know." Poppy frowned. "I'm not really in the mood."

"Aw, come on." He tugged at her arm. "Don't be like that, okay? Just think about it . . ."

The two of them wandered off together. I shook my head, sensing the start of yet another argument.

Just then Sara hurried toward me. "Hi, Nancy," she said in her soft voice. "I wanted to check on you. Are you okay?"

"I'm fine," I assured her. "Are you going to take a turn on the zip line?"

Sara shuddered. "No, not today."

"Have you done it before?"

"Yes, many times." She nodded. "But it seems different now somehow."

I couldn't help feeling sorry for her. She seemed even more shaken than Poppy or any of the others. "Different?" I said.

She hesitated, glancing up as Sarene glided past overhead. Then she shrugged. "It's silly, I guess," she mumbled so quietly that I had to lean forward to hear her. "It's just, well . . .".

Once again, she paused. "Yes?" I prompted, curious now. Did she know something she was afraid to say?

Finally she looked up and met my eye. "I just wonder," she said. "Do you think—could Casa Verde be—be cursed? With all that has happened . . ."

"Cursed?" I echoed. "What do you mean?"

"It is supposed to be a wonderful place for green living and fun and beauty," Sara said. "But maybe it is not meant to be that way."

"What do you mean?" I asked again, suddenly flashing back to what Phyllis had said. "Are you talking about the stuff Juliana did? Or is there something else? Maybe rumors that Casa Verde isn't as 'green' as it's supposed to be?"

Sara bit her lip and stared at the greenery all around us. I waited, holding my breath. Did she know something?

Before she could speak, Alicia called her name. "Excuse me," Sara murmured, turning and rushing off toward her boss.

I slumped down, disappointed. Had Sara been about to tell me something important? Or was she just upset by witnessing my fall after everything else that had happened lately?

I had no idea. But I was going to do my best to find out.

I didn't have another chance to speak privately with Sara before we left the zip line place. In fact, by the time the bus dropped us off in front of the resort, I hadn't found out much more at all. If anybody had a sense of who might have messed with that zip line, they weren't saying.

"Oh well," I said with a sigh as my friends and I entered our room. "I guess I can try to talk to people again at dinner. But I'm starting to wonder if we're

going to be able to solve this in the next day and a half."

"Never mind that," Bess said, setting her bag down on a table. "I'm just glad we're all back safely."

"Me too." I slung my own bag onto my bed. It fell open, and I noticed a slip of paper inside. "Hey, what's that?"

"What's what?" George kicked off her shoes and flopped down onto her own bed.

"This." I plucked the paper out of the bag and let out a gasp. "It's another note!"

I showed it to my friends. It was written in the same block letters as all the others. This one was short and sweet, consisting of a single word:

DEEPER.

TIME IS RUNNING OUT

The next morning I woke up stiff and a little sore, my body's delayed reaction to the fall from the zip line. Every time I moved, I was reminded of how close I'd come to being badly injured or killed the day before. Who would be willing to go that far to make his or her point? It was hard to imagine any of our suspects doing something as serious as sabotaging the zip line. Well, except maybe Phyllis—we didn't know her well enough yet to judge her character, and she did seem kind of unhinged.

"I just can't stop thinking about it," I confessed

to my friends at breakfast after Bess had to ask three times for me to pass the sugar. "What if the line hadn't broken when it did? Or what if someone else had gone first—maybe Robin?"

"But it didn't, and they didn't," George pointed out. "And come to think of it, that second part was no accident."

Bess pursed her lips thoughtfully. "She's right, Nancy. The director pretty much insisted that you go first!"

I had to admit that the fall had wiped that fact out of my mind until now. "Is that suspicious?" I wondered. "It's definitely a little odd. Why me?"

"Well, he said it was because you were right for the test shot," Bess said. "Which is true—you look like Kat, although she's a little taller than you. But if they only needed a blond stand-in, they could've just as easily picked me. My hair is closer to Kat's color than yours is."

"True." I touched my strawberry blond hair, glancing over at Kat's platinum tresses at the next table. "And come to think of it, that Michaels guy was on the phone right before he asked me to go. Maybe I should talk to him—see if whoever he was talking to suggested he send me up first."

George's eyes widened. "You think someone could be targeting *you* now?"

"Maybe. What if someone's figured out I'm investigating this whole mess?" I shot a look at Frankie, who was loudly holding court across the dining room. "It's not like that's a big secret, thanks to certain people."

Bess grimaced. "True," she agreed. "Maybe whoever it is thinks you're getting a little too close to some answers."

"But why would that director guy listen to a random person?" George protested, reaching for another slice of toast. "I mean, if you're talking about Juliana or whoever . . ."

"Why not?" Bess argued. "He's the *assistant* director, remember? He's used to taking orders. Besides, Juliana is the boss's niece." She shrugged. "Anyway, it's worth checking out."

"Definitely," I said. "It's not as if we have a lot of other leads right now."

We hastily finished eating, then headed out to look for the assistant director. Just outside the dining room we ran into Hildy, who told us she'd seen the crew heading off down the main path through the resort.

"Come on," I said to my friends as we went in that direction ourselves. "Let's see if Mr. Michaels is with them."

George nodded. "Okay. But I—hey, is that Sara?"

Bess and I looked where she was pointing. Just ahead, the young woman was crouched down over something on the trail. When she heard us coming and glanced up, I saw that her face was covered in tears.

"What's wrong?" Bess cried, rushing forward.

"Don't come too close! I'm trying to keep it calm until Alicia gets back." Sara sniffled and moved aside a little.

That was when we all saw the bright red parrot lying on the ground in front of her. Its beautiful plumage was in disarray, and there were several deep-looking cuts on its wings and back. The bird was clacking slowly in distress as Sara held it down.

"Oh, wow," George said. "What is that, some kind of parrot?"

"It's a *lapa roja*," Sara said. "Um, I mean . . ." She paused, obviously too upset to think clearly in English.

"A scarlet macaw?" Bess guessed.

Sara nodded gratefully. "Yes, that's right. They are very endangered in the wild."

"What do you think happened to it?" I asked, eyeing the wounds.

Sara stared at the bird, seeming uncertain how to answer. Just then Alicia appeared behind her. She was out of breath and carrying a large wire cage.

"Got it," she called to Sara. Glancing at us, she nodded a quick hello. Then she set the cage down and opened the hinged top.

"Is it going to be okay?" Bess asked.

"I hope so," Alicia said grimly. "We need to get it back to the office so we can medicate it and get a better look at its wounds."

"How did it get hurt?" George asked.

Alicia shrugged. "It was already down when Sara found it. Maybe it had a run-in with a predator, or more likely got tangled in the wind turbines."

"Really?" I couldn't help being a bit dubious. Admittedly I wasn't a veterinarian or any other kind of bird expert. But those injuries looked more like wire cuts to me than anything else. Would a wind turbine cause that type of wound?

Alicia was bending down to help Sara grab the bird. As soon as Alicia touched it, it let out a squawk and kicked out at her with its curved claws.

"Careful!" Sara exclaimed.

"Rats," Alicia muttered. "Just realized I forgot to grab my gloves." She glanced up at us again. "Listen, could one of you do me a favor?"

"Anything," I said immediately.

"There's a pair of heavy leather gloves lying around in the vet hut somewhere." The biologist waved a hand back the way she'd come. "Should be either on the examining table or somewhere nearby."

"I'm on it."

I took off in the direction of the veterinary hut. It

wasn't far, and soon I was pushing through the front door, which was standing partially ajar.

The gloves weren't on the exam table, so I glanced around the room. I didn't spot the gloves right away, but I did notice something else.

What's that? I thought, stepping around the table and staring at something on one of the counters.

It was a ragged piece of material that looked like thick, stiff cardboard—or maybe more like leather. My mind flashed to that missing chunk from the leatherback turtle's shell. This looked about the right size and shape to be that missing piece. But how had it ended up here?

Did Alicia or Sara find it somewhere on the grounds and pick it up? I wondered. *Or could one or both of them be involved in what happened?*

Just then I spied the gloves sitting on another counter nearby. I grabbed them and took off, my mind spinning with what I'd just seen.

Once Alicia had her gloves, it didn't take long for her and Sara to lower the injured macaw into the cage. The two of them headed off, carrying the cage carefully between them, and my friends and I headed the other way.

As soon as I was sure we were out of earshot, I told Bess and George about the leathery chunk. They were just as surprised and confused as I was.

"Could either of them really be involved?" Bess exclaimed. "They seem so nice—and so dedicated to animals and the environmental mission here!"

"I know. But that's exactly the point." I shrugged. "What if they've discovered that those Internet rumors are right? What if Casa Verde isn't as green as it claims? Maybe they want to expose that." I glanced over my shoulder in the direction the pair had gone. "I mean, that bird didn't look like it had tangled with a wind turbine to me. If this place is supposed to be such a well-designed, eco-friendly reserve, what would injure it like that?"

"Well, it could've been a predator like Alicia said." George seemed thoughtful. "But I wonder if—"

She clammed up so suddenly that I looked over at her in surprise. When I did, I saw that Frankie had just appeared behind us.

"Hello, hello!" she greeted us, hurrying to catch up. "What are you three up to?"

She sounded suspicious. Had she overheard part of our conversation?

I decided to play dumb. "We were just wandering around looking for the film crew," I said. "We thought it would be fun to watch them do their thing."

"Oh." She still looked a little skeptical. "I just saw them over by the botanical display garden."

"Thanks! See you later." I turned and hurried off with my friends right behind me.

Luckily, Frankie didn't follow us. And a few minutes later, we found the film crew exactly where she'd said they were. Unfortunately, the assistant director wasn't with them. The main director, Harvey, was watching as Kat, Deirdre, and Pretty Boy frolicked among the flowers. Well, Kat and Deirdre were frolicking, anyway. Pretty Boy was mostly snapping at bugs or trying to eat the plants.

"Hi," I said, walking over to Harvey. "Where's your second in command today?"

The director shot me a surprised look, as if wondering who exactly I was and why I was speaking to him. "Michaels?" he said. "He's in San Jose this morning. Meeting with someone from Green Solutions HQ."

My heart sank. So much for questioning the assistant director!

Rejoining my friends, I filled them in. "Bummer," George said. "Guess there's no point hanging around here, then. Not unless we want to watch Deirdre and company make even bigger fools of themselves, that is."

"Let's not and say we did," Bess said.

I nodded. "Maybe we should try talking to Enrique. He seemed really upset about what happened with the zip line. It's possible he knows more than he was letting on."

I knew it was a long shot—the taciturn chef hadn't exactly been willing to open up to us so far. But I was running out of ideas as well as time.

We wandered back into the main building. Breakfast had ended some time ago, however, and the kitchen was deserted.

"No Enrique," Bess said. "Want to see if Cristobal knows where he is?"

"I have a better idea." George was staring hungrily across the room at Enrique's computer.

I shot a quick look around. There was still nobody in sight. "Go for it," I said. "But be careful!"

George hurried over and sat down at the computer. Bess and I stood behind her, by turns watching her work and keeping an eye out for anyone passing by.

George started surfing some travel sites on the Web. Within minutes she'd pulled up information on all the flights and buses around Costa Rica.

"Here we go," she said, tapping the screen. "Looks like someone by Phyllis's name did fly into San Jose the day before yesterday from someplace called Puerto Limon."

"I think that's a town on the Caribbean side," Bess said. "Just as she said."

I nodded, shooting a look over my shoulder. The sound of voices was drifting in from the direction of the main lobby. It was only a matter of time before Cristobal or someone else walked past the kitchen door and saw us in there.

"Let's leave it at that," I whispered. "We don't want to get caught in here."

"Hang on." George was already clicking through to a different site. "I just want to check on some of the stuff she was saying about Green Solutions."

Soon she'd found several different blogs criticizing the company. Most of them also mentioned Casa Verde. We didn't have time to do more than skim, but the gist seemed to be just as Phyllis had said—that Casa Verde had cut corners to make itself look more green than it really was.

"Interesting!" Bess said. "Looks like Phyllis isn't completely crazy after all. Or at least she might have been telling the truth about why she's here."

I nodded. "Okay, now you'd really better log off before we get caught," I warned George. "Too bad— I'd love to do a little research on Adam and Poppy, and see if we can figure out what motive either of them might have."

"I can do a quick search," George offered, fingers already poised over the keyboard.

"Not now," Bess whispered. "Let's get out of here.

Maybe we can borrow Frankie's laptop later or something."

"Yeah, right." I rolled my eyes. "Only if we tell her everything we know and promise to give her full credit if we ever do figure things out."

George chuckled and moved the mouse to click off. But then she paused. "Hey," she said, staring at something on the screen. "What's this?"

She clicked an icon that had been minimized in the corner. It enlarged and filled the screen.

"Looks like it's just Enrique's e-mail in-box." Bess shot another glance over her shoulder. "Close it and come on—I think I hear someone coming!"

But George was already clicking on one of the e-mails. "Check it out," she said. "Think this is one of those love letters Juliana told us about?"

Despite my anxiety about being caught, I couldn't resist a closer look. "Doesn't look like it," I said. "This isn't addressed to Virginia. It's to someone named Cassandra Samuels."

"Close that right now!" Bess sounded scandalized. "We shouldn't be reading his private e-mails!"

George ignored her, clicking on another note. "'Dearest Cassandra,'" she read. "'My beloved, I cannot wait until the moment when I can see your beautiful face again. . . .' Yep, definitely love letters! And definitely *not* to Virginia!"

"Unless they set up secret names in case Cristobal came across the messages or something," I suggested. "They could do that, right?"

"Sure." George shrugged. "All they'd have to do is set up a separate e-mail account under the fake name. But why disguise her name and not his?"

"And why write to each other in English rather than Spanish?" Bess pointed out.

"Is there a way to find out where these e-mails are going and coming from?" I asked George.

"I can try to trace the ISP." George leaned forward. But before she could do anything, we heard footsteps in the doorway.

"Hey!" Enrique exclaimed from behind us. "What are you girls doing in here?"

AMONG THE PREDATORS

We all stared at the chef for a second, like deer caught in the headlights. George was the first one to recover.

"Sports scores," she blurted out. "We were, uh, just checking on how our favorite team did yesterday."

Enrique stared at her. "Oh," he said.

I winced, waiting for him to ask what team or sport or score she was talking about. But he didn't, instead he just glanced toward the computer screen.

Shooting a quick look that way myself, I was relieved to see that George had clicked away from the e-mails. Had he seen what we were looking at before she did? I hoped not.

"Sorry," Bess spoke up in her tactful way. "We were going to ask if we could borrow your computer for a sec, but since nobody was here, we didn't think you'd mind."

"Of course not," Enrique muttered. However, he still looked a little suspicious as he politely shooed us out of the kitchen.

Outside we hurried away around a corner. "That was close!" Bess said. "Do you think he suspects what we were doing?"

"Probably not. I just hope he's not computer-savvy enough to trace back and see what we were looking at." I glanced at George.

She shrugged. "He doesn't seem like the type. But you never know."

Just then we heard Cristobal calling for attention out in the main lobby. Heading that way, we saw that most of the other guests were already gathered there.

"The bus will be leaving for the crocodile tour right after lunch," Cristobal announced.

"Crocodile tour?" Robin clapped her hands, looking excited. "That sounds cool!"

"It does sound kind of cool," George said to Bess and me. "Are we going?"

I sighed. "Why not? We're certainly not learning anything useful around here."

"I think Enrique still suspects we were up to something this morning," Bess whispered to George and me. "I just saw him shoot us a funny look."

The three of us were in a large flat-bottomed boat floating down a wide, slow-moving river. Most of the other Casa Verde guests were on board as well, though Sarene had again chosen to stay behind at the resort. Enrique was once more leading the tour in his brother's place, and once more seemed less than thrilled about it. Alicia and Sara were also there, along with the entire film crew, including the assistant director, who had returned from San José just in time to join us. Kat and Deirdre were taking full advantage of being trapped in a small space with the crew, vamping and prancing for the cameras for all they were worth.

"Watch out," Adam called out as Kat held Pretty Boy up near the edge of the boat to look at a toucan perched in a tree on the shore. "You'd better keep a tight hold on that dog. Looks like crocodile bait to me!"

Kat shot him an incensed look and immediately pulled Pretty Boy in closer. "What a horrible thing to say!" she cried. Then she buried her face in the dog's fur. Or rather, the polka-dotted sunbonnet currently covering it. "Don't pay him any mind, baby."

"Speaking of crocodiles," Alicia spoke up, "if you'll all look over the left stern, you can see a couple of them now."

"Really? Let me see!" Frankie hurried closer. She snapped a few photos with a fancy-looking camera. "Wow, my editors are going to eat this up!"

Robin gasped and pointed. "Look! There it is, Mom! Oh, wait—it just went under the water."

"Don't worry," Sara told the little girl with a smile. "There's a spot farther upriver where we're almost guaranteed to see plenty of crocodiles."

Hildy chuckled. "A real croc hangout, eh?"

"Something like that," Sara agreed. "And even if they're acting shy, we brought along some chum we can use to attract them or bring them closer to the boat."

She gestured toward a few buckets sitting at the back of the boat. I'd glimpsed into them earlier, just long enough to see that they contained bloody, fly-encrusted chunks of meat.

"Aw, man!" Adam called out. "You mean that's not a snack for us?"

He laughed loudly at his own joke, though only a few of the others chuckled along politely. I'd already noticed that he seemed to be in an especially good mood that day, though Poppy was her normal quiet, reserved self.

The boat's operator continued steering up the river. As we drifted lazily along, Alicia pointed out various species of birds flying overhead or perched on shore, along with the occasional monkey, sloth, deer, or ocelot. We also saw a few more crocodiles, though they mostly ducked underwater when they heard the boat coming. It was an interesting tour with tons of gorgeous scenery and some truly fascinating wildlife, but I couldn't help being distracted. We would be heading home tomorrow, and I was still no closer to figuring out who was leaving those notes—and why.

Still, I did my best to enjoy myself, trying to remember that I might never have the opportunity to visit Costa Rica again. Even so, I never quite stopped thinking about the case. When I found myself at the back of the boat with Alicia, I decided to take advantage of the semiprivate moment to ask her about that chunk of turtle shell I'd seen in the vet hut.

Alicia was leaning back, her elbow propped on the low edge of the boat. She squinted up at me. "Oh, yes," she said casually after she heard my question. "Sara found that in the mud outside the main building. We figure it must have torn off while whoever put that turtle there was trying to get it inside. We're going to drop it off at the restaurant the next time either of us is in town. They should be able to glue it back on."

"That's good," I said automatically. The biologist's story made perfect sense.

Maybe that chunk of shell isn't a clue after all, I told myself uncertainly. *Unless Alicia's lying, that is.*

I shot her a look. She'd tilted her face back and closed her eyes, smiling and seeming to enjoy the feel of the sun on her skin. She certainly didn't *look* like a woman with something to hide. . . .

There was a sudden commotion at the front of the boat. Alicia's eyes snapped open and she sat up. "Oh, good," she said. "We're here."

"Where?" I asked, but she was already standing up and hurrying to the middle of the boat.

I stood up too. The boat was gliding into a lovely, still, open section of water. Birds were chirping and monkeys were calling in the trees along the shore. Everyone was oohing and aahing at the beautiful sight.

"Okay, people," Alicia began cheerfully as the operator cut the motor, allowing the boat to drift to a stop. "If you'd like to turn and look to the east—"

"Excuse me," Adam broke in, jumping to his feet. "Sorry to interrupt. But I just can't wait any longer to do this."

"Do what?" Frankie called out.

Adam ignored her. Stepping over to Poppy, he dropped dramatically to one knee, grabbing her hand. "My darling," he intoned. "This trip together has made me realize that I can't imagine life without you. Would you do me the honor of becoming my wife? Please, babe?"

Poppy just goggled at him for a moment. She looked surprised but also kind of annoyed. Finally she burst into tears.

"I told you not to do this!" she cried. "I've been trying to tell you, I don't care how romantic a story this would make. You know I'm just not ready!"

A few people had gasped or let out exclamations during Adam's proposal. But now everyone on the boat went silent, with nobody seeming to know where to look or what to do.

"Awk. Ward," George murmured, sidling up beside me.

Poppy had yanked her hand away from Adam and was glaring at him through her tears. He was glaring back.

"I can't believe you're embarrassing me like this!" he hissed. "What more do I have to do?"

"How about listening to me for a change?" she exclaimed.

There was more, but like everyone else, I was doing my best not to listen. That was no easy task on a boat that suddenly felt way too small and crowded. In any case, I now understood the couple's weird behavior. It didn't have anything to do with the mystery. Just an ardent would-be groom and a not-yet-ready-to-be-a bride with cold feet.

That explains all the arguments and tenseness between them, I thought ruefully. *It probably even explains why Poppy disappeared into the bathroom for so long yesterday. She was probably crying or something—now that I think of it, she kept her sunglasses on for the rest of the trip, even while she was in the shade, probably trying to hide her red eyes. . . .*

"Never mind, you two," Bess spoke up at last, stepping forward to put a comforting hand on Poppy's arm. "It's clear to everyone here that you guys love each other. Maybe you just need a little more time to work things out, hmm?"

"Or maybe I need better taste in men," Poppy snapped, wiping away her tears with the back of her hand.

"Babe!" Adam protested, looking stricken.

"There, there." By now Hildy had hurried forward to join Bess. She patted Poppy's arm, shooting Adam a sympathetic look. "Let's not say anything we don't mean . . ."

She and Bess steered them both toward the back of the boat, still murmuring soothingly. "Wow," George said as she watched. "That was crazy."

Deirdre was standing close enough to hear her. "He was probably just trying to get into the ad," she said with a sniff. "Some people will do anything for their fifteen minutes of fame!"

I poked George hard in the ribs before she could respond. This was no time to add one of their sniping matches to the mix. "Anyway," I said loudly, "what were you about to say before, Alicia?"

Alicia cleared her throat, looking relieved. "I was just going to tell you all to take a look over there if you want a closer view of some crocs," she said. "See? There's one there, and another right there . . ."

When I looked the way she was pointing, I gasped. A couple of large crocodiles were floating just a few yards off one side of the boat!

"Look, there are more over there!" George exclaimed, jabbing her finger ahead of us.

"She's right!" Robin cried. "They're all around us!"

"Creepy," Kat declared, hugging Pretty Boy closer.

She had a point. It was a little eerie to look out there and realize that we were completely surrounded by dozens of the huge, prehistoric-looking predators floating silently in the murky water. But it was kind of cool at the same time.

George pulled out her camera and started snapping pictures. Most of the others were doing the same, including Robin.

"Ooh, look!" the little girl cried after a moment. "That one's yawning!"

"Where?" Frankie exclaimed, shoving her way to that side of the boat.

Almost everyone else also crowded over that way as well, including the camera crew, who were filming away. Kat hung back a little, still seeming nervous about letting Pretty Boy get too close to the edge. But just about everybody else did their best to get a good view. I found myself shuffled to the very front of the group, my knees pressed against the low side of the boat.

I watched the crocodiles for a moment, then decided to give someone else a chance at a front-row view. "Excuse me," I said, beginning to turn around.

But just then I felt hands on my back, giving me a hard shove. I was already a little off-kilter from trying to turn on the gently bobbing boat, so that was all it took to make me lose my balance.

My shin clunked the edge of the boat as I scrabbled helplessly at the air, trying to grab on to whatever I could. But there was nothing there. With a scream I felt myself tumbling over the side of the boat.

Splash! I hit the water and went under.

10

SCARE TACTICS

As I said before, it takes a lot to scare me. But being dumped into a tropical swamp with dozens of crocodiles all around me? Yeah, that'll do it.

I flailed my way back to the surface, squinting to keep the algae and assorted slime out of my eyes. To make matters worse, I realized that although the boat's motor was off, it was still moving, drifting slowly with the current. By the time I looked around, it was already a dozen yards behind me.

"Nancy!" Bess shrieked. "Quick, everyone—she fell overboard!"

I was vaguely aware of the commotion on the boat as the guests realized what had happened. But much more of my attention was taken up by staring at the crocodiles in front of me. They looked even bigger at eye level.

The closest one eyed me with lazy curiosity. Its head raised a little higher in the water, and it glided closer.

I gulped, frozen with terror. Behind me, I heard the boat's motor come to life with a roar. But I knew it was already too late. There was no way it could turn around and get back here before that croc reached me. . . .

"Hang on, Nancy!" Sara's voice called out over the sound of the motor.

A second later I heard a series of small splashes. The crocodile turned its head. For a long moment it just hovered there, staring off to the side. Then it began gliding away in that direction!

I went limp, almost bobbing beneath the surface again. But then I realized this could be my only chance. . . .

Spinning around, I struck out for the boat. It was coming toward me, and as I reached the side, a dozen arms stretched down to pull me back on board. I collapsed on the floor, gasping. Bess grabbed a towel and tossed it over me, while Hildy started checking me over in her maternal way. The others just stared at me, shock written all over their faces.

"I already knew you were, like, a magnet for trouble," Deirdre commented, sounding shaken. "But this is crazy! First that zip line and now this?"

"Yeah." Frankie nodded. "You really need to be more careful."

"Whoa," I blurted out as soon as I regained enough breath, ignoring Frankie's comment. "That was close! What made that croc leave me alone?"

"It was Sara's quick thinking," Alicia said, her voice shaking. "She grabbed some of that chum and tossed it overboard in the other direction."

Sitting up, I could see a frenzy of crocodiles still fighting over the bloody chunks of meat. I shuddered, feeling sick as I realized how close I'd come to being the object of that food fight myself.

"So you're sure you have no idea who shoved you?" George asked me for the umpteenth time.

I shook my head. My friends and I were sitting by the pool back at the resort, doing our best to recover from my close call. As soon as we had been alone, I'd told them about feeling those hands on my back. Unfortunately, neither of them had seen who had shoved me.

"I'm guessing whoever it was, it's the same person

who tampered with the zip line," I said. "After all, we were with just about the exact same group. And I guess this also makes it clear that I'm the target."

Bess shivered despite the late-afternoon tropical heat. "It certainly looks that way," she agreed.

"This lets out Sarene as a suspect," George said. "She wasn't along this time."

"And Juliana and Phyllis, too," I added. "Plus, there were no unknown people on board except the boat's driver, and we're all pretty sure he stayed at the controls the whole time."

Bess nodded. "I remember seeing him still in his seat right before I heard the splash," she said. "I just wish I'd been looking over in your direction at the time instead!"

"Me too." I sighed. "We can probably cross Poppy and Adam off the list, though. I'm pretty sure they were still huddled at the back of the boat with Hildy at that point. So there go all our likely suspects." I bit my lip. "Still, even if Alicia and Enrique seemed ready to believe it was an accident, I know it wasn't."

"Speaking of Enrique, do you think he could've done it?" Bess suggested. "Maybe he was trying to shut us up after he caught us at his computer earlier."

George brushed at a mosquito that was buzzing around her head. "Maybe. But only if he's the one who's been leaving those mysterious notes and stuff."

I squinted up at the cloudless blue sky, doing my best to puzzle through what little we knew. "But why would the note writer pull something like that?" I mused aloud. "I thought she wanted us to look deeper into things here at Casa Verde, not scare us off completely."

"Okay, let's be logical about this," George said, finally squashing the mosquito against her arm and then flicking it away. "Who could have shoved you today? It wasn't the boat driver. Poppy and Adam are out. Hildy was back with the not-so-happy couple, so she's out too—not that we ever suspected her in the first place. And I'm guessing Robin probably isn't some kind of kid psycho, either. So who's left?"

"Enrique, like I said," Bess replied. "Alicia and Sara. The camera crew."

"Frankie, Kat, Deirdre," I supplied, trying to recall who else had been on the boat.

George brightened. "Hey, what if it was Deirdre?" she said. "We already know she's evil."

"Get real." Bess rolled her eyes. "Deirdre may be a lot of things, but I don't think she'd actually try to murder Nancy."

"Don't be so sure," George muttered darkly.

I ignored her, still pondering our dwindling list

of suspects. "Let's not get too focused on today. We need to think about everything that's happened so far and who had the opportunity," I suggested. "And I'm starting to think we should start way back at the beginning."

George shot me a look. "You mean the stuff that Juliana did?"

"Juliana never confessed to any of it," I reminded them, feeling unsettled. "And most of our evidence was circumstantial. What if she's been innocent all along?"

"But Pretty Boy . . ." Bess began.

I nodded. "That's what keeps throwing me off too," I admitted. "But how do we know somebody else didn't dognap him, then plant him in Juliana's room to throw suspicion off themselves?"

"I guess it's possible," Bess agreed thoughtfully. "Okay, then starting from the beginning, we have our luggage disappearing. Then there were a couple of those mysterious notes about looking deeper. And, of course, Pedro getting drugged and Pretty Boy disappearing."

"I guess it's safe to say the camera crew is out, then," George said. "They didn't get here until way after all that stuff happened."

I stared out at the sparkling waterfall at the end of the pool. "They weren't here yet for the turtle thing either. And most of our other suspects were with us that whole day." I sighed, frustration welling up again. "It just doesn't make sense!"

"Maybe it does," Bess said. "Maybe Juliana did dognap Pretty Boy and do some of the other stuff. But somebody else did the rest, like the zip line and the shove today."

I nodded slowly, thinking over that theory. "The only thing that's clear is that somebody seems to have it out for Casa Verde," I said. "And after seeing that sewer pipe—and maybe that injured macaw, too— I'm starting to wonder myself."

"That brings us back to Enrique," Bess said. "He was at Casa Verde when the turtle appeared. And he was along with us today and also at the zip line place."

"Yes, but you could say the same thing about Alicia and Sara," George pointed out. "Well, except for the turtle part, since they were on the snorkeling trip with us."

Bess blinked. "Wait, are you sure? I know Alicia came, but I think Sara skipped that one."

"Yeah, I guess you're right," I said with a sigh. "But anyway, I think you may be right in thinking Enrique is about the best suspect we've got at this point. And it would make sense that he could be working with Juliana."

George looked thoughtful. "True. She could've been that mysterious voice on the phone, but either of them could have been the one luring us out into the jungle."

"And Enrique oversaw a lot of the construction of Casa Verde," I said. "I remember Cristobal mentioning it. So he would know if corners were cut."

"Yeah," George said. "Because he'd be the one doing it! So why would he expose his own wrongdoing?"

"Maybe he feels guilty? Or maybe Cristobal was the one who ordered the shortcuts—who knows?" Bess shrugged. "Anyway, it does kind of make sense that it would be Enrique, given that Nancy is his latest target. He could blame her for getting Juliana into trouble."

"Enrique could have taken our luggage." I started ticking things off on my fingers. "He could have left the notes. He could have tampered with the zip line. He could have pushed me overboard today."

"What about the dognapping incident?" Bess put in. "Enrique wasn't with us on that trip."

"No, but that makes it even more likely. It would have been easy enough for him to steal the drug from the veterinary supplies and put it in Pedro's water bottle," I pointed out. "And he could have followed us in a separate vehicle and waited until Pedro passed out so he could snatch Pretty Boy."

George shook her head, still looking unconvinced. "But then why would he want to show us that sewer pipe?" she asked. "I think Bess is right—we might be dealing with two culprits here. Maybe someone is trying to expose problems at Casa Verde, and Enrique is trying to shut them—and us—up before that happens."

I thought about that for a moment. The theory certainly would explain why we were having so much trouble pinning all the problems on one person. Before I could reach any useful conclusions, however, we heard voices approaching.

It was the film crew. It turned out they were planning to make up the postponed pool scene now that the graffiti had been cleaned off the waterfall.

"Over there, please, ladies!" Harvey called to Kat and Deirdre, who were dressed in their bikinis again. This time Poppy was nowhere in sight; I guessed she had more important things on her mind than fixing Kat's outfit or touching up Deirdre's makeup. By the time we'd docked earlier, she and Adam had appeared to have reached a tentative truce, though their future had still seemed very much up in the air.

As Kat and Deirdre giggled and struck a pose, I noticed the assistant director standing back behind the cameramen, watching the scene. That reminded me that I'd never had a chance to talk to him earlier.

"Be right back," I told my friends. Then I hurried over to Mr. Michaels. "Hi there," I greeted him.

He blinked at me. "Hello. I hope you've recovered from your swim with the crocs earlier. Amazing how many ways the wildlife around here have to try to kill you, isn't it?"

"Yes, it's quite a place. But listen, I was just wondering a few things."

His gaze was already wandering back to the pool, where Kat and Deirdre were now pretending to sunbathe while Pretty Boy scampered around barking. "Yes?" he said, sounding a little impatient.

"I remember Harvey mentioning that he's a freelancer, but I think he said you work directly for Green Solutions," I went on. "How long have you been with the company?"

He shrugged. "Long enough," he said. "Why?"

"I just had some questions about how they do business. You know—like how closely they would have worked with the Arrojos to design and build this place, or—"

"Well, you've got the wrong guy, then." He cut me off with a dismissive look. "I do the publicity stuff for GS, that's all. The rest is none of my business. Now, if you'll excuse me . . ."

He hurried over to adjust one of the lights, then

went to talk to Harvey. I shrugged and headed back to my friends.

"Dead end," I told them. "He says he doesn't know anything."

Bess checked her watch. "It's almost time for dinner," she said. "Let's go back to the room and change."

George and I agreed, though I couldn't help feeling unsettled and disappointed. Time was running out. Was I going to have to admit that I'd finally found a mystery I just couldn't solve? It was certainly looking that way.

I was trailing behind my friends, lost in thought, when we reached the room. But I snapped out of it when I heard Bess gasp loudly.

"What?" I asked, rushing over.

She pointed. There was a note lying on the nearest bed. Racing over to grab it, I saw that this one was scrawled in a much more casual hand than usual. It read:

COME TO THE VET HUT
IF YOU WANT YOUR ANSWERS.

George was looking at it over my shoulder. "Well, what are we waiting for?" she exclaimed. "This could be our last chance to solve this thing!"

We all turned and scurried back out of the room. Moments later we skidded to a stop in front of the vet hut. The door was ajar, but nobody seemed to be around.

"Let's go," I said, stepping forward to push the door the rest of the way open.

When I peered inside, things were dim and quiet. The only thing out of order was a straw hat lying on the floor a few feet inside the door.

Bess saw it too. "Alicia and Sara never wear hats like that," she said, stepping inside. "They always wear those green ones with the Casa Verde logo on the front and their names embroidered on the brim."

"Think it's a clue?" George asked.

"Not sure what a straw hat's supposed to tell us," I said as I followed them in, though I couldn't help recalling that the mystery figure I'd seen at the zip line place had been wearing a similar hat.

Meanwhile, Bess bent down and picked up the hat, then jumped in surprise. There was a small, bright yellow frog sitting on the floor where the hat had been. Its throat pulsed rhythmically as it stared up at us.

"Oh, look!" Bess exclaimed. "There was a cute little frog hiding under it."

"Cool!" George stepped forward for a better

look. "Here, I think I can catch it . . ."

She slowly bent closer to the tiny, jewel-like creature. But just as she cupped her hands as if to grab it, there was a clatter of footsteps behind us, followed by a loud gasp.

"*Stop!*" someone yelled. "Don't touch that frog!"

CONFESSION AND CONFUSION

I spun around in surprise. Sara was standing there, her normally tanned face as white as a sheet.

George had frozen in place. Sara leaped forward and pushed her aside.

"Stay back," she ordered. "Let me catch it."

She grabbed a long-handled net from the counter nearby. Wielding it expertly, she scooped up the little yellow frog and dumped it into an empty tank, which she then covered carefully with a piece of mesh.

Finally she turned to face us again, still looking pale and very serious. "That was close," she murmured, collapsing against a counter.

George frowned. "What's the big deal?" she demanded. "We weren't going to hurt it if that's what you're so worried about."

Sara stared at her. "No, that's not what I was worried about." She glanced into the tank, where the frog was looking around at its new surroundings. "That's a golden dart frog. Most people consider it the most poisonous vertebrate in the entire world."

I gulped, glancing at the innocent-looking little creature. "Really?"

"Really." Sara nodded.

Bess looked stricken. "I think I remember reading about those," she said. "They have this toxic stuff on their skin that, like, attacks the nervous system or something."

"Yes, a frog of this species generally has enough toxin in its skin to kill at least a dozen humans," Sara said.

"Whoa!" I looked at George. She was speechless for once, seeming horrified by her close call. My mind flashed briefly to what Mr. Michaels had said earlier. It seemed he was right. There really *were* a lot of ways the wildlife around here could kill you.

"But wait." Bess scrunched up her face, looking puzzled. "I didn't think there were any of those supertoxic species in this part of Costa Rica. I know there are other slightly less poisonous frogs here, but—"

"No, you're right—this particular species is found only in Colombia," Sara confirmed. "There's no way it just wandered in here on its own. Someone must have released it on purpose."

With that, she burst into tears. I was even more startled by that than by the revelation about the deadly frog.

"It's okay," Bess said, instantly going into soothing mode. She hurried over and patted Sara on the back. "We're all okay. George didn't get close enough to touch it, thanks to you. No harm done."

Sara shook her head, still crying. "It's—it's not that," she sobbed. "I just never thought things would go this far. . . ."

I traded a confused look with my friends. What was she talking about?

"This frog—I think it was a message for me," Sara choked out through her tears. "I never thought Enrique would do anything like this. I was only trying to help. . . ."

Now I was starting to catch on. "Wait. It was you, wasn't it?" I asked her as several puzzle pieces finally slid into place in my head. It was all making sense now. "You were the one who left the other notes. You must have found out this resort wasn't as green as it's supposed to be and you wanted to get the word out. Is that it?"

Sara's sobs slowed and she shot me a nervous look. But finally she sighed and nodded.

"I couldn't just stand by and do nothing," she said. "Not with Casa Verde passing itself off as a model of environmental living."

"Of course," Bess murmured, catching on as well. "We always did notice how passionate you are about the environment."

George still looked a bit confused. "But how could you have done all the bad stuff?" she asked. "It's not like you could carry that sea turtle in on your shoulders."

"I had help from some friends in town," Sara said with a sniffle. "But please, do not blame them. They are innocent, and thought it all merely a prank against the Arrojos for disrupting our quiet life with more tourists. They meant no real harm. And I wanted only to make a statement that could not be ignored."

"Did the same friends help you steal our luggage too?" I asked.

She nodded, sniffing again. "I told them only to hide it, but they went too far," she said. "I am very sorry your things were ruined."

After that, the rest of it came out. Sara was the one

who'd dognapped Pretty Boy, though she assured us that she would never have hurt him.

"What about poor Pedro?" George challenged her. "He could have been hurt if he'd had too much of that tranquilizer you gave him."

"I am familiar with the drug," Sara insisted. "I knew exactly how much to put in the water to make him nod off without harming him. And do not worry—it would not have acted fast enough to cause an accident. He would have had time to pull over when he began to feel drowsy."

I nodded, feeling at least a bit comforted by that. But I still had more questions for her.

"Was Juliana involved in this at all?" I asked.

"No, I merely needed a place to hide the dog when I feared I might get caught." Sara shrugged. "Juliana, she has a wealthy family. I knew they would make sure she did not get in too much trouble."

Was it my imagination, or did I catch a whiff of sour grapes in her voice? Then again, maybe it wasn't surprising. The two of them were both locals, and close enough to the same age to have been in school together. Who knew what history they might have?

"I do feel terrible for spooking Cristobal's horse that day," Sara put in. "I never thought a seasoned trail horse would react so strongly. I only wanted to scare Cristobal a little to make him realize he cannot control everything, which I thought might convince him to listen to me."

I'd nearly forgotten about that incident. During a beach ride earlier in the week, a small mechanized toy had sent the horse that Cristobal had been riding into a panic, which had set off several of the other horses as well. There had been a few dangerous moments, though in the end, nobody had been badly hurt.

"Well, what about Nancy?" George put in hotly. "You could have killed her with that stunt today! Not to mention the zip line thing."

"What?" Sara's brown eyes widened with horror. "But I did not do either of those things! I would never purposely put anyone in such danger! I swear it!"

The three of us traded skeptical looks. After everything she'd just confessed to, Sara's word didn't mean much.

"Really," she insisted, her eyes filling with tears again. "Don't you remember? I was the one who lured the crocodiles away from Nancy so she could be pulled to safety!"

"That's true," Bess admitted. "But how do we know you didn't just do that to throw off suspicion?"

"Never mind," I said. "Right now I have a more important question. Why did you do it?"

I turned to Sara, pretty sure I already knew the answer. But I wanted to hear it from her.

She glanced over at the frog again, looking somber. "I have been here from the beginning," she said. "Even longer than Alicia or most of the others. I have seen the shortcuts that were taken in the building of this place. The environmental ravages that have been hidden from most eyes."

"Like that sewer pipe?" Bess guessed. "Were you the one who led us out there?"

Sara nodded. "I tried to call the investigative-reporter woman first," she said. "But she did not answer her phone, and when I remembered hearing her saying that Nancy had assisted her in the earlier investigation, I decided to try your room next."

Letting the issue of my "assisting" Frankie pass, I pressed on. "So who else knows about this?" I asked. "Are Cristobal and Enrique both in on the corner cutting?"

"I am not sure about Cristobal," Sara said, staring again at the poison dart frog. "I tried to speak with him about it when I first noticed that the builders were not following the specs on the original plans. But he brushed me off, seeming to think I knew nothing about it." She shrugged. "As for Enrique, I am certain he is aware of everything. I have seen him near the problematic areas enough to have no doubts. The sewer pipe, the wires that injured that bird . . . Yes, he knows."

I couldn't help feeling sad to hear that. Enrique

was an odd duck, but he had seemed nice and sincere beneath his shyness. "How could he have betrayed the whole mission of Casa Verde that way?" I mused aloud. "Possibly even to the point of deceiving his own brother?"

George shot me a grim look. "I bet I know the answer to that," she said. "Money. It makes people do crazy things."

Sara sighed. "I think you are right. At least it is the only conclusion I have been able to reach. Enrique must have gone behind the backs of Green Solutions, and probably Cristobal as well, so he could pocket the extra cash."

Her mention of Green Solutions made me remember the encounters with Phyllis. "I wonder if this explains those Internet rumors," I said. "Maybe someone else found out that things weren't kosher here, so to speak, and blamed the consulting company."

"Unless Green Solutions was involved in all this too," George said.

I nodded. "It's possible, I guess. But we'll have to leave that to someone else to figure out." I glanced at Sara. "In the meantime, I think you need to tell Cristobal the truth. All of it."

She looked kind of queasy, but nodded. "Yes," she said. "I think it is time."

I hesitated, still not sure whether to believe her

claim that she hadn't been responsible for the most dangerous stunts. Looking into her eyes and hearing her talk about her reasons for doing what she'd done, I couldn't quite find it in myself to believe she could be capable of attempted murder. But if not her, then who? Was it possible both incidents could have been accidents? Thinking back to the feeling of those hands on my back, I didn't think so. But I decided to let it drop for now.

Soon all four of us were heading into the main building. Sara hadn't said a word on the walk over; I could only imagine what she was thinking. Bess, George, and I had been mostly quiet too, aside from a little small talk about packing for our flight home the next day. It was hard to believe our stay at Casa Verde would soon be over. Despite all the problems, it had been the trip of a lifetime.

"Oops," Bess said, glancing at her watch as we passed the dining room windows and heard voices inside. "I just realized we're late for dinner."

We hurried into the lobby. As we did, the sounds from the dining room were drowned out by other voices—raised, angry ones. Turning the corner, we saw Cristobal and Enrique glaring at each other in the hallway outside the kitchen. And a moment later, Cristobal let out a roar of anger and swung his fist at his brother's face!

OUT IN THE OPEN

"Cristobal, no!" Sara cried, leaping forward. We hurried after her. Enrique had ducked quickly so that Cristobal's fist had missed its mark. And both men seemed startled enough by our sudden arrival to stop what they were doing.

But Cristobal still looked furious. "Do not interfere!" he cried. "My brother needs to learn a lesson about deceiving me!"

I winced, guessing that he'd figured out what was going on at Casa Verde at about the same time we had. "Please, Cristobal," I said. "Let's just talk about this. What happened?"

Cristobal glared at Enrique. "A crazy American woman just came to visit me," he said, his normally jovial voice sounding icy. "She all but forced me to come along with her to look at what she claimed some locals had told her were nonrenewable insulation and other materials in one of the buildings. I went merely to humor her—but to my surprise, her accusations were correct!" His fists clenched again. "How could you, Enrique? I had suspicions before, as you know, but to have my face shoved in it by a total stranger . . ."

He switched to Spanish, continuing to yell at Enrique. But it didn't matter. I'd heard enough to guess the rest. It sounded as if our friend Phyllis had been talking to the locals and had finally found someone to give her some dirt. It also seemed that some of the intense conversations I'd witnessed between the brothers had involved this topic as well. Had Cristobal paid more attention to Sara than she'd thought, or had he seen or heard something else that had raised questions? I supposed it didn't really matter.

I turned to Enrique, who was standing there stoney-faced. "Listen," I said, "for what it's worth, I'm sorry I accused Juliana before. I realize now she didn't do anything wrong."

That made Enrique's face crumble. "Juliana," he muttered, burying his face in his hands. "No, she knew nothing of any of this. I always knew she was innocent."

After that came a flurry of explanations. Sara stepped forward and, her voice shaking, admitted what she'd done. Cristobal looked shocked at first, but acknowledged that he should have listened to her in the first place.

Then it was Enrique's turn. He confessed to everything that Cristobal had accused him of doing. "It was all me," he said, his face twisting with guilt. "I did it for the money. I was fully responsible for it all—yes, some local construction people did the actual work, but they aren't to blame. They did only what I ordered." He shot his brother a haunted glance. "I am sorry, Cristobal. I do not know what else to say."

By now the other guests were trickling out of the dining room, attracted by all the raised voices. There were a few minutes of chaos as the guests all got caught up. When Kat found out that Sara was the one who'd dognapped Pretty Boy, she freaked out loudly and at great length.

"Just chill out," Deirdre snapped at last, apparently as fed up with her cousin's hysterics as the rest of us were. "The little twerp is okay, isn't he? So it's over."

"But he must have been so scared!" Kat wailed, clutching the Chihuahua closer, much to his obvious discomfort. Pretty Boy wriggled around and bared his teeth, clearly frustrated that Kat was squeezing him too tightly for him to be able to bite her.

"It's over now," Hildy said soothingly. "And everyone is all right. Some people just get a little carried away when it comes to saving the environment, that's all. There are worse crimes in the world."

"True enough," I agreed, thinking not only of Sara but of crazy Phyllis as well. Then again, I realized that maybe I shouldn't think of her as crazy. After all, she'd been right about the resort, even if Enrique had turned out to be the culprit rather than Green Solutions.

In any case, it seemed the mystery was finally solved. But Sara still wasn't confessing to the zip line or crocodile incidents, which was sort of troubling. And thinking back to her shock at seeing that poisonous frog, I couldn't help wondering how it had gotten there. Was it Enrique? And had he been the one to push me overboard? It was unsettling to realize that I might never know the answers. . . .

I was still thinking about the remaining unanswered questions as I packed my things the next morning. Bess was bustling around our room as well, though George was lounging on one of the beds with half her clothes still strewn around the place.

"Hurry up," Bess chided her cousin. "The bus leaves for San José in, like, an hour."

"That's plenty of time," George said with a yawn. "I want to stay in vacation mode as long as possible."

Before Bess or I could respond, the door to our room flew open with a bang. Standing in the doorway was Juliana.

"Please!" she cried out, sounding upset. "I heard what happened, and you have to help me! My father is innocent—I know he is!"

I winced, realizing that Enrique must have just told her the whole story. "I'm really sorry, Juliana," I said, setting down my bag. "For everything. Especially accusing you of all that stuff. I know now that you didn't do any of it."

She waved a hand as if shooing away a fly. "That's not what I'm talking about," she said. "My father loves nature too much ever to do anything to hurt it. If what he just told me is true, he must have been duped into going along with it somehow! Probably by this mysterious American girlfriend of his!"

Huh? I traded a confused look with Bess. Even George sat up on her bed and stared at Juliana.

"American girlfriend?" I asked. "What do you mean?"

"Those letters—the ones I told you about? On his computer?" Juliana said urgently. "I took another look and saw that they are not to Aunt Virginia at all! There are dozens of them to and from someone named—"

"Cassandra Samuels," George finished. "We saw them too."

"Then you know!" Juliana rushed over and clutched her by the arm. "You know she must have put him up to this!"

"Listen, Juliana," Bess said kindly, sneaking another peek at the time. "We're heading home soon; I think maybe you should talk things out with your father."

"I tried!" Juliana sounded more desperate than ever. "He just keeps saying he is responsible. But I know this woman in Chicago must have something to do with it!"

"In Chicago?" George echoed. "How do you know that's where she is?"

Juliana shrugged. "She mentions it in one of the letters," she said. "I was not able to read them all, but I saw enough." Her eyes flashed angrily. "I cannot believe he allowed this woman to get him into trouble! And now he is taking the blame instead of fighting back—"

She was interrupted by a sudden, loud scream from somewhere outside. "What was that?" Bess exclaimed as the scream came again.

I was already pushing past Juliana to the door. All four of us raced outside, where we found a horrifying sight. Sara was standing on the pathway in the main garden, her head completely engulfed in tiny swarming insects!

Others had emerged out of the buildings by then. Among them was Alicia, who let out a cry of horror. "Army ants!" she cried. "They're attacking her face! *Dios mio!*"

"Out of the way." Cristobal had appeared as well. Racing over to Sara, he scooped her up as easily as if she were a kitten. Then he ran off down the path with her cradled in his arms, hardly seeming to notice as some of the ants swarmed over his arms.

I realized what he was doing. "The pool!" I yelled over my shoulder to my friends, already dashing after him. "He's going to toss her in the pool to get them off her."

Ten minutes later, it was all over. The pool trick had worked pretty well—Cristobal and Alicia had jumped into the water with Sara, washing away the ants as quickly as they could. Then the two of them had accompanied her to Violeta's medical station for treatment. As Sara had passed by us, I'd had to look away—her face was already swelling from the multitude of bites.

"Do you think she'll be okay?" Bess asked, staring after them.

"I hope so. At least they got them off her fairly

quickly." I glanced over at the others still gathered around. Most of the guests were there. "Did anybody see what happened? How'd those ants get on her head like that?"

"They were in her hat," Frankie said in a trembling voice. "I was standing right here when she put it on. They just came swarming down over her face! It was horrible!"

I shot a look at my friends. Their expressions said that they were both thinking the same thing I was: There was no way this was an accident. The timing was just too suspicious.

Someone must have found out that Sara was the one who had exposed the not-so-green side of Casa Verde, I thought grimly. *Probably the same someone who tried to scare me off the case by messing with the zip line and turning me into crocodile bait. Was it Enrique? Or could someone else be responsible?*

Either way, it seemed this wasn't over. Yet what was I supposed to do about it with our plane leaving so soon?

I wasn't sure. But Nancy Drew never leaves a case unsolved. And no matter what it took, I was going to see this one through to the end. . . .

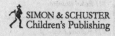

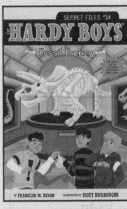

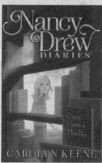

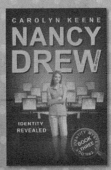
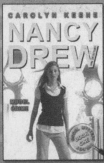
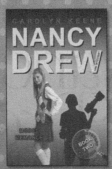

NANCY DREW

Available from Aladdin